FREE
FALL

For Tim —
I can't pretend that
this is Grunwaldian, or even
(honors) Bravian. However, I
think you'll like the hero's "moral"
preparedness —
Thanks for my virgin
trip through sower country
[signature]

J. D. REED

FREE FALL

A NOVEL

DELACORTE PRESS / NEW YORK

Published by
Delacorte Press
1 Dag Hammarskjold Plaza
New York, N.Y. 10017

Manufactured in the United States of America
Second Printing—1980

Designed by Oksana Kushnir

LIBRARY OF CONGRESS CATALOGING IN PUBLICATION DATA
Reed, J D 1940–
  Free fall.

I. Title.
PZ4.R3238Fr [PS3568.E366] 813'.5'4   79-15776
ISBN 0-440-02724-1

I would like to thank Mark Kram, Mike Taylor, and Dan Wigutow for their ideas and their support.

This book is for Phoebe and Alicia

Put me on a highway
and show me a sign;
take it to the limit
one more time.
                —The Eagles

FREE
FALL

1

THE DESCENT

Free fall. Four thousand feet on the altimeter strapped to his wrist, the hands of it stable for a moment before the wind caught him, before gravity took up its chore and began pulling him to earth, two seconds of silence in which he was almost free of all demands and dues, and then the rush of air belled out his cheeks, the wind whistled through his helmet and goggles, and his hand tightened on the D-ring of the parachute. The hands of the altimeter began to move backward as he stretched into a semispread-eagle position, keeping his feet tucked in to balance the heavy waterproof sack strapped to his waist. Back toward earth, accelerating.

He rolled over in the fall to sit on the wind and look up at the Northwest Orient 727 wheeling away from him, the rear exit stairway from which he'd stepped just a moment before still dangling from the plane, making it resemble a huge, aluminum hornet heading back to the hive as it turned north, back to Sea-Tac International.

The plane had not, as he feared, veered toward him, to jockey him into one of those great, sucking engine cowlings, nor was it going to circle, marking his landing position. The bomb would take care of that. Three thousand feet. He flipped over again. He tried to smile against the rip of the wind.

Below him the snow-dusted carpet of green took on shape, acres of Douglas fir began to separate into distinct trees, endless spires pointed at him, on the Washington-Oregon border, Thanksgiving afternoon. To the north Mt. St. Helens, ancient and volcanic, stood iced, its crusted coat of old snow catching the rays of the setting sun, washing it a pale red, as if some huge animal had bled to death there long ago. And from its base stretched out two thousand square miles of the Pinchot National Forest, a huge preserve of larch, pine, fir, volcanic boulders, lakes as shiny and flat as smashed coins visible through the cedar tangles. To the south he caught a glimpse of the Columbia River, where the Sasquamash Indians, fat on sweet Tokay, tended the last of the salmon ladders, and the tepee-shaped sawdust burners smoked wetly near the lumbermills of Camas. It was wild country that belonged to the deer and the wolverines. And humans inhabited the edge of it, living in the shadow of the nameless wild into which he was now accelerating, hurtling. Fifteen hundred feet.

He pulled the D-ring and the chute tore free with a hiss of nylon. He braced for the great groin-jerk as the straps of the harness bit into him and he traveled swiftly upward, floating on a thermal. He swiveled to see the 727, now just a flasher on the northern horizon: They couldn't possibly see him, as he floated helpless, over the cold forest. Even time began to drift.

If below him the air were hotter, if the green foliage exploded into broadleafed plants and tangles of vines, it could be Vietnam toward which he descended, as he had done five years before, down toward the green unreality of the Cambodian border, toward the relentless VC and the rabbitty ARVN platoon; down toward the leeches, the muddy rivers, the snakes, heads bobbing death on the ends of pikes, blood on sacks of spilled rice, the helicopter wreckage, the senseless certainty of death and killing.

But this was Washington, cold and American, a precisely defined wilderness on the map and in the heart. The light was fading as the tips of the tall firs came closer to his feet. He tugged the shroud lines, angling faster toward a break in the forest ceiling, and before his body sliced through the treetops, he saw lights in the barns near Ariel, Washington, and then the branches stung his face and his legs and he banged hard against a tree trunk and jerked to a stop, twenty feet above the darkening ground below.

He listened for a moment to his own breath, saw it steam from his mouth, and he shivered, swinging gently in the wind like a huge leaf; smiling, hugging the bundle strapped around his middle. He tied a parachute line to a stout branch to belay to the ground, his fingers numbing in the wind.

Field Inspector William Gruen of the Federal Aviation Agency watched the jump-suited FBI agent sprint into the knee-deep layer of foam under Northwest Flight 44. He began to skid, wagging his arms for balance, and landed hard on his ass, sliding right under the belly of the plane.

A Seattle Police Tactical Squad cop next to Gruen snickered. "Those assholes will do anything to be first, won't they," he breathed through the dark plastic face visor under his blue helmet.

"That's what happens when you give a CPA a tommy

gun." Bill Gruen didn't like the FBI. It was fine with them if he stood around in cold hangars for a month at a time, watching technicians try to figure out why three thousand fragments of metal and plastic that used to be an airplane had flown into a mountain, but when the time came for real action, like a skyjacking, they stepped all over his toes and popped out of drawers with press releases and tin-horn patriotism.

The FBI man in the combat suit had recovered and was scampering up the rear stairway of the plane, covered with foam like the Pillsbury doughboy.

The sea-side taxi ramp at Seattle-Tacoma International Airport was a beehive of activity. In the chilly darkness of Thanksgiving night two trucks of arc lamps had lit up the corner of the airport as if it were a movie set. The Seattle police's bomb disposal truck was parked a quarter of a mile away, where Lieutenant Rico and his boys were sweating over five pounds of plastique. The airplane was ringed by helmeted Seattle policemen shouldering riot guns and rifles as they shifted from foot to foot in the cold wind that blew in off the Sound. The FBI man, accompanied by several of his comrades and a few policemen, FAA investigators, and an assistant DA, were inspecting the interior of the airplane. The crew, shaken but unharmed, were being tended to in a nearby motel, and what appeared to Gruen to be a young Indian in a three-piece Pierre Cardin suit faced a battery of lights, talking rapidly into a windproof microphone.

". . . after the unidentified skyjacker had received the cash in small bills and the parachutes he had demanded on the ground in Denver, he kept his word and released the rest of the passengers, taking off with the crew. He apparently jumped from the plane's rear-exit stairway somewhere between the Idaho border and Seattle, although authorities here will not pinpoint the location . . ."

Pinpoint was hardly the word, thought Gruen, in the two thousand square miles of wilderness into which this son of a bitch had dived. He ran a large, calloused hand through his short-cropped graying hair and headed for the airplane. Bill Gruen was not so tall that he stuck out in a crowd, but he gave the impression of height. Perhaps it was because at the age of forty-seven he had retained the slender waist and wide shoulders of his youth, promoted by a five-mile run each morning. There was something compact and coiled about Gruen, like a bunch-muscled middleweight fighter, that lent him stature even against taller men. Or perhaps it was his wide-set blue eyes under the gray, flying buttress eyebrows. In airports, where he spent most of his working days, Gruen was often taken for an off-duty airline captain—he had that look of control, confidence, and capability. Hardly anyone would have taken him for an FAA inspector, a man who checked out cargo-hatch doors and ran down civil pilots who violated federal air space.

Before he "retired" into the agency, Gruen had been a front-line master sergeant in the Army Rangers, the Green Berets, and had won a chest full of ribbons and a few scars in the jungles of Vietnam. Then they brought him home to train troops and to show off at enlistment centers. Put out to stud. It sat wrong with him, and he'd taken the line job at the FAA, hoping for action. This was the first he'd seen in a year that had the sound and the smell of it. He approached the airplane like a dieter walking up to a smorgasbord—slowly and with all the savor in the world.

"Bill," called a dark form jogging across the tarmac. "Hey, wait up." A lumpy figure jogged into the circle of bright light around the plane. Lieutenant George Rico wore a padded flak apron and a face shield tilted onto his curly black locks: bomb squad high fashion. He leaned against the railing of the plane's stairway and stuck an unlit cigar in his mouth.

"I don't want to go in there," he rasped, nodding at the stairway, "and drop this one on them."

"What one?" asked Gruen.

Rico puffed on his cigar, even though it wasn't lit. "Your boy stuck up the candy store with a cap gun."

"What?"

"The bomb's a fake, Bill. It's five pounds of kid's modeling clay, electrician's tape wrapped up to look like wires and a Big Ben alarm clock. There aren't even any detonator caps. The bastard walked right through the X-ray and metal detectors in Denver when he got on that plane, and no one could have noticed anything unusual. This guy's a cutie."

Gruen began to laugh, a hearty, deep sound. "I'll be damned. We can't even get him for armed robbery. The FBI will shit bricks. They'll have to warrant him on traffic violations."

"That's why I don't want to go tell them." Rico chewed the cigar violently.

"But I do, Rico, I do." Gruen trotted up the stairs into the plane after Rico's padded figure. He wouldn't miss that for the world. In the meantime it was dead dark outside, deer season was underway in the state of Washington, and some cowboy was running around in a vast woods with $750,000 in small bills and it wasn't even armed robbery.

J. R. Meade leaned against a tree trunk in the darkness, shining a penlight at the compass needle. He was on his course. Some women thought Meade had a kind of handsomeness, but most folks would pass him by as just another young man who worked for the phone company, or on a surveying crew or as a carpenter's helper. The only thing that arrested the close observer were his eyes. There was a twinkling delight operating behind his ordinariness, an indication of intelligence and wit one didn't usually find in a power-line crewman or a cowboy.

J. R. Meade was thirty-one years old. His brown hair was cut short, his body as hard as a soldier's. In the camouflage combat coverall and canvas and rubber jungle boots he resembled some escapee from guerrilla warfare suddenly plunked down in the great Northwest. Meade checked his compass heading a second time and blinked out the penlight. He waited a moment for his night vision to return, using the old army trick of straining one's eyes to look out to the sides, dilating the pupils. Soon he could make out the trees, the larger rocks, and the shapes of the hills. He pushed off from the tree and walked silently into the dark. He had fashioned the waterproof canoeing sack of money into a backpack with lengths of parachute shroud lines. He had no weapon except the razor-sharp, double-bladed survival knife, a souvenir of five years as a Green Beret, winning hearts and minds in the Mekong and the highlands of Vietnam. He moved through the dark as comfortably as an infantryman wore a flak vest. Alone in the wilderness Meade was at home.

As he padded on the soft carpet of larch and pine needles, he thought how perfectly it had gone from the beginning, and he smiled in the darkness, lines crinkling around his eyes. From the time he handed the stewardess the note as the plane sat on the taxi ramp in Denver, through the demand for the money and the three sport parachutes, the delivery after three sweltering hours on the ground, the release of the passengers, to the phony flight plan for Mexico, to locking the crew in the flight deck and jumping, it had gone as smoothly as any military operation. No one even scratched.

And now he moved toward a Jeep full of supplies that he'd hidden in the forest three weeks before. Meade had driven into Pinchot back in September as a fierce-eyed Sierra Club type, on the lookout for pollution, gum wrappers, smoke, and aluminum foil. He hadn't had to check in at the park gate, for the tourist season was over. In corduroy shorts and a goose-down vest and big, mountain-climbing boots, he'd gunned the Jeep up the gravel roads and jounced along a weedy, stump-filled fire trail and carefully covered the Jeep with brush and netting. He'd backpacked out, stubble-bearded, wearing eyeglasses. He doubted if any ranger or local type in Ariel, the small town he'd passed through, remembered him; he looked like one of the growing army of folks who were determined to enjoy the goddamn wilderness, whether they liked it or not.

He stopped again in the darkness and the compass's magnetic north swung into his line of march, sixteen degrees off true north, where the Jeep would be found. He heard the small scrabbling sounds of the night's feral animals busy at their hunting and eating; ground-hugging, sharp-snouted mammals. They would have done well on Tokyo's Ginza or on Broadway, restlessly moving all night to satisfy their appetites and retiring sleepily at dawn.

And then he heard the movement of something larger; an irregular sound, the crack of a branch. Meade stood stock-still, his arm tensing as it rested against the shaft of the survival knife. He heard a chewing noise, like a giant at a bowl of Rice Krispies. He let his muscles slump. Deer. Night-browsing mule deer crashing around eating, staying out of the sight of the thousand deer hunters that would be up at false dawn, stalking.

Moonlight came through the clouds, thin and pale. Meade could make out the dark shapes of the deer twenty meters off through the trees. He was downwind of the radar-eared creatures. He clapped his hands once and the small herd bolted away, veering off into the shadows noisily. Meade moved out again, breathing easier. Contact had been made. He was back on earth, among mammals, carrying his loot and ready to get on with it.

The stewardess was pure Colorado, Gruen thought. She drank her coffee black in the private lounge off the lobby of the Seattle Airport Inn, where the crew had been stashed for the night, to be "debriefed," and mostly to be kept away from the television people and the reporters until the FBI and the FAA had their story straight. She was a golden girl, taller than Gruen in her cowboy boots, Levis, and checked shirt. Her honey-colored hair bounced down over her shoulders. But you could see the ranch life in her hands as they cupped the mug of coffee. They were weathered hands with big veins, powerful hands roughened by reins and soap and fenceposts. Her name was Pat and she smoked Camels. And she wasn't one of those semihysterical twits who always seemed to end up stews, the ones who live in packs in singles apartments drinking Kahlúa and going at sex like Olympic swimmers.

"How long have you been a stew, Pat?" Gruen lit her Camel and she held his wrist steady with one of those big rough hands.

"Four years, Mr. Gruen. I never thought I'd stay this long."

The FBI man played with his tape recorder and shifted restlessly in his chair next to Gruen. Amenities were not taught at the FBI Academy.

"Run through the whole thing for us, everything. What this guy said, what was the name on the flight list, Carl Perkins? We need to know everything we can about him."

She told the story without embellishment, from the time "Carl Perkins" had taken his aisle seat in the first-class section. There was nothing unusual about him, no special physical characteristic, nothing weird or foreign. He'd simply gotten up as the plane had taxied out to the runway and come over to her jumpseat near the door to the flight deck, carrying his small gear bag. She'd told him to return to his seat, but he'd calmly and firmly told her that he had a bomb in his bag and he wanted the airplane to turn out of line and park on the unused southeast taxiing ramp. He unzipped his bag and showed her the bomb with the ticking clock. She used the intercom to tell the pilot. The man had stood at her side, his hand on her shoulder, letting her peer into the bag.

The crew had followed the prime rule of skyjacking: They obeyed, calmly and soothingly, relaying Carl Perkins' demands to ground control.

"We're taught to treat these people as mentally disturbed, or as political crazies. But this guy wasn't like that at all. I was kind of babying him. But I guess I was too obvious or something."

"What do you mean?" Gruen stared at her hands.

"He caught on right away. He said, 'Relax, honey, I just want the money.' Then he told me to get all the tourist-class passengers off the rear stairway."

That was one of the many things that had perplexed the gathering tribe of FBI, FAA, and Denver police that morning, when they saw three dozen passengers milling around under the tail of the aircraft. It intrigued Gruen. The normal pattern of skyjackers was to hang on to everybody in the plane for bargaining power.

"Did he say why he did that?" asked the FBI man,

leaning over the table toward the stewardess like a Dober-
man on a hot scent.

"He made a joke of it. He said he only had a small
bomb and he could only blow up first class and the crew."

Gruen began to think that Carl Perkins was either a
real bad mental case or a man with a lean sense of humor.

"What did he do while he waited for the money to be
delivered?" asked Gruen, making notes on the back of
his gas-bill envelope.

"He mostly sat and played with a piece of string."

"Played with string?"

"Yes. Like tying knots. Real fancy ones."

While Carl Perkins, or whatever his name was, played
boy scout, Gruen thought the FBI and Northwest officials
made the crucial decision to go ahead with the payment.
Marksmen couldn't get a bead on him. And Carl Perkins
had given them a three-hour deadline to deliver $750,000
in small bills, and three sport parachutes. The FBI, as
usual in such cases, got the Northwest officials to stall,
claiming that on a holiday such as Thanksgiving, the
banks were closed and it would take them quite a while
longer than three hours to collect that much money.

Carl Perkins had instructed the pilot to say that Northwest should Telex each of its ticket desks and have all
their cash, plus whatever they could borrow from other
airlines at their offices, flown to Denver on whatever
flight was available. Since it was a holiday, and since
Northwest in this part of the country flew a lot of local
short-hop folks who paid cash instead of using checks or
credit cards, he knew they could get the money together
in time. In three hours he was going to set his timer and
blow the crew and first-class passengers to kingdom come.

Gruen had been amazed at the man's mind. What he'd
postulated was possible, and Northwest came up with
$685,447 in two and one-half hours, as Northwest flights

crowded the glide paths around Denver. The tactic also gave the FBI little time to record serial numbers. Carl Perkins was one smart skyjacker.

Pat brushed back her long hair and looked at Gruen. "Is that all?"

"Sorry. Thinking about all this. Listen, Pat, what did you think of this guy? What was he like?"

"He was a nice man, he . . ."

"A *nice man*? A *nice man*?" sneered the FBI man.

Pat sat up straighter. "He was a lot nicer than half of the damn businessmen that fly. He never threatened me physically, didn't even play grabass. He didn't bother anyone. I got the idea that he'd never set off that bomb. He was a real steady guy. And good-looking in a way. I kind of liked him."

Gruen and the FBI man led Pat through the rest of the story. How the money and the parachutes were delivered. How he let the seven first-class passengers go. How he told the pilot to take off and fly a course of 381 degrees at twenty-one thousand feet.

"He kept checking his watch and looking out the window," Pat recalled, half-smiling. "Then he told me to call the pilot and get a reading on wind speed and direction on the ground. When he had that, he told me to tell the pilot to fly at four thousand feet in a right-hand circle, at 165 knots with full flaps. Then he said, 'Good-bye, Pat, don't take any wooden credit cards.' He locked me on the flight deck with the crew. He yelled through the door that he was wiring the bomb to the door handle, so we had to stay on the flight deck, and that we had one hour before it blew up, so we had plenty of time to get to Sea-Tac and get off. That scared hell out of all of us. Could I have a light please?"

Gruen held out a match, watching her as she sucked deeply on the cigarette.

The FBI man shifted restlessly in his chair. "Did you smell it?"

"What?" Pat looked at him incredulously.

"Did you smell the bomb? See, plastique has a distinct odor, a strong one. That's how you can tell it from modeling clay, the odor."

Pat smiled, a big toothy Western grin. "Wait a minute. You mean that guy had a phony bomb?" The FBI man stared uncomfortably. Pat laughed heartily. "Oh, shit. Excuse me, but that's great. He seemed like the kind of guy who could pull that off. That's like those old movies where the convict carves a gun out of a bar of soap. Damn!"

"Look, Pat," Gruen smiled confidently at her, "I agree it was a great trick, and he didn't hurt anyone. 'Carl Perkins' is one great practical joker, but he still committed grand larceny and scared the hell out of everyone. We can't all just laugh it off. The next guy who tries that may have a real bomb, and a worse sense of humor. We've got to get him. Now, you haven't even told us what he was wearing, or how his voice sounded or anything. Think carefully. For instance, did you see him at all after he locked you on the flight deck?"

She thought for a moment, still smiling. "Well, sort of. When he was pretending to wire the bomb to the flight-deck door—at least the police when we landed said the bomb wasn't wired—the door clicked open a few inches, and I was standing by the engineer's chair, and I saw something, I think."

"What was it?"

"I saw his foot and his leg and I thought it was kind of funny."

Gruen perked up. "What was funny?"

"Well, he'd changed clothes. He had on these funny boots. They looked like they were canvas and rubber.

They are army color, you know, olive. And the sides were high and made of cloth, and the bottoms were rubber. I remember thinking that they were weird boots for parachuting. I've done a little skydiving, and we always wore big leather boots, for the landing shock, you know."

Vietnam jungle boots, that's what this big, pretty girl was describing, Gruen realized. They were made of canvas and rubber because leather rotted within days in the fetid humidity and the brackish water of tropical Asia.

"And his pants were different, too," Pat continued. "He'd been wearing khakis when he got on, but he'd changed while we were on the flight deck, I guess. He had on camouflage pants. I couldn't see the rest of him." The FBI man stared at his tape recorder as if it held the key to the magical kingdom.

Gruen began to feel the same electricity as when he'd been tracking VC in Nam. The signals, the ground signs, were coming clearer. Carl Perkins, or whatever the hell the guy's real name was, had been Special Forces in Vietnam. Gruen was sure of it. The jungle boots and the camouflage. And the only troops that parachuted in Nam were Green Berets. The terrain was too rugged and the war too local and hidden for big airborne troop drops. A man who parachuted in jungle boots was Special Forces. And Gruen had been Special Forces . . .

". . . then we saw the light go on indicating that the rear stairway was down and locked, and then we continued into Sea-Tac," Pat was telling the FBI man when Gruen focused again. She massaged her forehead with long fingers. "Listen, I've really had enough for today, I've got to get some sleep. Can we start again tomorrow?"

They said good night to her, and Gruen walked outside the motel, where even at 1:00 A.M. traffic streamed by on the expressway toward Seattle. It began to rain. So he was a professional. Carl Perkins. A good Special Forces man, trained to think alone, to mount his own actions;

trained for survival, deception, trained to kill in a dozen ways. The FAA was going to need Gruen on this one. They couldn't keep him at a desk. He let the light rain fall on his face, and he began to whistle, heading for his car.

When the rain began J. R. Meade was very near the hidden Jeep. He'd found the marker he'd left on a boulder: *Donny & Debbi* in runny spray paint. In Special Forces he'd been taught to leave natural trail markers. If something went wrong on a mission, there might not be time to find some old Indian tree blaze, or a bent twig or a pile of stones. Make something large, something so blatant that no one would ever guess it was a trail marker.

He picked his way around the stumps in the fire trail as he moved up the hillside toward the Jeep. He clicked off priorities in the darkness. The Jeep should be safe. He'd covered it with netting and built a natural cover over it, but the possibility of discovery was always there: a curious park ranger inspecting fire trails, a game warden looking for a hidden, illegal kill, one of the local hunters sweaty with venality. They were possibilities that Meade was ready for.

When he judged his position to be about two hundred meters from the Jeep, Meade moved to the side of the fire trail, blending into the firs. He wanted to run to the vehicle, to tear the cover from it, gun it up, and roar hell-bent out of the park, get away before anyone could mount a search; drive all night and all day, running with the money. But the feeling passed. He steadied himself next to a thick tree trunk. He remembered that day in jungle training school in Cambodia, when the instructor, a rail-thin captain from West Virginia, told his small group of Berets, "You just don't *imitate* a tree, you *become* a tree." Meade hadn't laughed nervously with the rest of the group. He knew what the captain meant in a flash of understanding that made him think, weirdly, for a moment, that he had known that lesson all his life. And now it came so naturally to him, beaten into his synapses by several years of necessary practice, that as he stood in the Douglas firs, even a VC couldn't have spotted him.

"Oooooh. Aaaah."

Meade froze, his heart pounding. A human groan echoed through the woods. His mind raced.

"UUuuuhhh." Another voice. Two of them. His hand flashed to the knife. And then he heard the regular, familiar rhythm. Within one hundred meters of where he stood, people were making love. "Oh, God. Oh, fuck me. Oh." A woman's voice.

Meade almost burst out laughing. He'd been ready to kill as in Vietnam, where night sounds were never love and meant only terror and death. But this was the great Northwest and someone was getting laid in the piney woods. The rain dripped off his waterproofed, camouflage coverall, a comfort in the dark as he listened to the thrashings and moanings. He moved quietly and sat down farther back in the trees. His mind drifted back.

He thought of Doc Thou, of an afternoon when the love groans came from his own throat, hunched over the slat-thin whore in a wet hootch. Everything was the same temperature—the whore, the rain, the bed, the air. As he labored over her, the whore had looked out the window at the rain on the rice paddies, far away from him. It was one of those points in life which he remembered clearly; so clearly that the moment obscured whatever lesson, whatever turning point he thought it should contain.

His life was a series of lessons, it sometimes seemed, that were never tested. A succession of images that contradicted one another. Unless you found something, *invented* something to hang on to. He was luckier than most in that respect. He unslung the sack of money and gear from his back and checked the time. Two hours until dawn, and a pair of lovers were camped right on top of his Jeep. He heard heavy footsteps and the sound of a post-coital piss. The man couldn't have been more than twenty feet from him. It was curiously soothing in the darkness, another human, one who didn't even want to kill you, doing something so profoundly animal near you. The footsteps receded and Meade undid the waterproof bag, shoved the stacks of bills aside, and pulled out a plaid shirt, duck pants, hunting boots, and a Day-Glo orange plastic cap. When he walked in on these people in the morning, he'd be a hunter, a license pinned to the back of the shirt. Just a guy out for a walk, who'd left his gun back at his camp.

Gruen studied the pilot with more than a casual glance. It was always possible that he'd been in on it, but this guy seemed straighter than the road to Ariel. Robert Ramage was not a photogenic Pan Am captain, graying at the temples and exuding confidence like a banker. Ramage was Mexican, thirtyish, his face scarred with smallpox pits. It made Gruen immediately trust him.

"I never saw the man, Inspector," Ramage said, puffing on a pipe and sweeping his black hair off his forehead, "but he knew what he was doing, that's for sure. He relayed all his instructions through Pat—uh, that was the stew on the flight—"

"I know."

"So I didn't even hear his voice."

"What do you mean, he knew what he was doing?" Gruen played with a piece of white butcher's string. At the end of it was a large, complicated knot that at first looked like a tangle, but on inspection proved to be an elaborately convoluted job of tying. It had been found in the seat pocket where Carl Perkins had sat on the 727. He swung it in the air and looked at the pilot.

"Well, his instructions. He had us fly at four thousand feet, which is standard parachuting altitude, if you're military, that is, where the object is to get onto the ground quickly without getting shot up, and assuming that anti-aircraft fire isn't so heavy that the aircraft can get in that low."

"You know about military operations, Captain?"

The pilot grinned. "The way you've been looking at me, I should say I was in the Spanish-American War, Inspector."

"Nothing personal. I've got a job to do."

"Am I a suspect in this?" The captain's eyes were amused.

"I don't know just yet," said Gruen, trying to keep him off balance. "Tell me about your military service."

"I wasn't in Vietnam, I was in Cambodia. I flew for Air America, for 'the Store.' And several missions involved parachuting. That's how I happen to know what was on that man's mind."

"You flew for the CIA?" Gruen wondered what Ramage was trying to tell him. That he had nothing to hide?

"Everybody said that Air America was involved in lots of illicit activities, but I never saw any of it. And I never saw any opium. We were supposed to be involved in the international drug trade, but it was all rumor. I flew propaganda missions. Leaflets to Saigon, an occasional politician or village leader from one place to another. But sometimes we had to parachute a political into Nam. That's how I know about the guy who skyjacked the plane."

"You think he was military?" Maybe all these signals were invented to throw him off, Gruen thought. But he'd checked the airline personnel schedules and it would be very hard for anyone to figure out when a certain crew, a stew, and a pilot, would be on the same flight together. He still felt that "Carl Perkins" had acted alone.

"He also knew what he was doing," said the pilot. "He had me fly at 160 knots, which is about as slow as you can go at that altitude and stay maneuverable in a '27. The guy knew about the aircraft. And he had me fly into the wind, and he asked for wind speed and direction on the ground."

"Why do you think he was military? Why can't he be just a weekend skydiver?"

"That's difficult. Even though I couldn't see the guy or hear his voice, it was the sequence of instructions, the language, I guess."

"Like what?" Gruen was getting the feeling again. Carl Perkins was Special Forces from Nam. His scalp prickled.

"Like talking in knots and meters. He could even have been a Navy flier."

"You think he could have been Special Forces?"

"A Green Beret? Hell, I guess so. Those guys know everything and then some. And they'd be crazy enough to pull off something like this."

"What do you mean?" Gruen stiffened.

"Oh, you know, who the hell would go through that training and run around in the jungle strangling VC with piano wire and eating snakes unless they're crazy?"

Gruen stared a moment at Ramage. He decided against telling him that he had been Special Forces, and that he never felt saner. It was interesting that a man sensitive about his own nationality could so chauvinistically describe Gruen's branch of the service, but the crazy reputation of the Berets had done as much good as harm. Gruen swung the piece of string with its strange knot that had been retrieved from the seat pocket where Carl Perkins had sat on the Northwest flight.

"Maybe we *are* after a crazy," Gruen said.

"One thing's for sure, Inspector, you're not after a *stupid* crazy." Ramage took his pipe from his mouth and laughed loudly, his white, square teeth glinting like piano keys.

As the battleship gray of false dawn spread out behind Mt. St. Helens to the east, J. R. Meade had completed his transformation from efficient skyjacker to deer hunter. He was now, according to the best fake ID cards money could buy in Toronto, one Mason Roberts, a roofing carpenter from Walla Walla, Washington, out for a week of deer hunting in the Pinchot National Forest, where hunting was allowed only after a lot of experts had done a herd population count and determined that there were too many deer to survive the snow-bound winter high in the hills.

Meade sat against a tree trunk where he'd spent the night two hundred meters from the hidden Jeep and closer still to the now-discernible campsite of the nocturnal lovers. He could make out their small, nylon pup tent pitched under the branches on the opposite side of the fire trail, just far enough into the shadows of the previous night to have been hidden in the darkness. Meade adjusted the wire-frame glasses that completed his hunter's outfit. They itched his nose. The best disguises, he'd been taught in sapper's school, were the most natural ones. False beards and mustaches, hair dyes, contact lenses that changed eye colors, were too obvious, even glaringly useless. A little cotton in the cheeks was fine unless you had to eat, eyeglasses were okay. Hats were the best, for they obscured the shape of the head. Wearing clothing that was either too small, or in Meade's case, too large, also changed the shape of the body, distorting people's observations.

Meade studied the lovers' campsite. The tent was a backpacker's model that weighed at most two pounds. It collapsed into a lightweight, compact bundle for hiking. Near the tent, two big, fifty-pound capacity backpacks strapped to magnesium frames rested against a log; a sack containing food was slung high over a branch ten meters away from the tent against the possibility of night animals looking for grub. They were hikers, woods freaks, who were probably too young to realize that they'd better get their asses out of the front lines while the annual deer slaughter was underway. There were still hunters around these parts who wouldn't mind bagging a backpacker or two instead of a mule deer.

Meade thought with a smile that it was surely strange the coincidences waiting for a person in the wilderness. In thousands of miles of wild country these kids had camped and humped within touching distance of his hidden Jeep. True, it was a natural camping spot, on an open fire trail with good drainage against the frequent rains at this time of year; that was one of the reasons he'd chosen it, but there were hundreds of fire trails in the forest. Maybe they'd been attracted by his trail marker, a declaration of love to compare to their own passion.

Meade got up, stretched, and moved silently back into the woods another fifty meters to stay out of sight of their camp. When they were up, he'd wander in, a deer hunter out on the trail, and talk a spell, maybe learn their plans.

So far, no one had been hurt in this escapade, and Meade didn't want to start it with a couple of kids. Half the idea of this thing was to do it cleanly, without a drop of blood spilled. He was convinced of his own powers of persuasion. If these kids planned to stay put for another few days, he knew ways to change their minds. Meade knew that the manhunt would start soon now, and he had to get clear of the forest with its six narrow road exits.

He settled down by a boulder, rested his back against it, and waited as the sky lightened and the birds began their morning calls. A gentle rain began to patter and hiss in the pine forest. Meade's mind twisted back to six years before when another rain had woken him in the wilderness, but that time it had been jungle. He'd woken with the rain on his face.

He was lying on the thick branch of a tree near the Ho Chi Minh Trail, one of the stretches that wandered through the thick jungle into Cambodia. There was no trick to sleeping in trees, only letting the body remember its former arboreal life. If you moved in the night, primal instinct made you reach out for your branch. On that morning he'd woken to the sound of voices. Staring up at the thick tangle of branches and vines that obscured the blazing sun and slate-colored sky of Asia, he heard them speaking Vietnamese, sprinkled with sing-song French. It was the Viet Cong platoon that had been pursuing him for a week as he ran southeast toward his own lines, if the shifting collection of villages and roads could be called a "line."

A week before, confident and hard-minded in his jungle fatigues and green beret, Meade had squatted much like the VC below him, breakfasting with the platoon of ARVN troops that he had led on sapper missions against underground caches of VC supplies along the trail. Small, frightened brown men, looking ridiculous in big American steel pot helmets and almost overpowered by the M-16s, his platoon had become increasingly frightened when villagers told them the VC had sent a special search group, their best, out to get them. The results would not be quick, clean deaths. And that morning, without a word, the ARVN, avoiding Meade's surrendering gaze, had stood up and quietly dropped their rifles, shucked their helmets, and walked off into the elephant grass toward the jungle. They'd turn back into peasants, Meade supposed, back to black pajamas and straw coolie hats, to trot along the roads past the VC and the NVA back to wherever they came from, to reenlist and get sign-on pay, and go off with some other American "advisor" to pull the same stunt if the going got rough. Even as they left him, five hundred klicks from nowhere, alone in the goddamn jungle, Meade had to smile. They were savvy little bastards. That was how you survived twenty years of war.

Meade ran for a week through a dream of hell—the punjab sticks smeared with excrement, the leeches, the rivers of muck he waded to obscure his trail from the fast-closing VC platoon. He even gnawed on bamboo like a goddamn panda at one point.

And when he'd woken that morning on a tree branch somewhere in the vastness of Asia, listening to those thoroughly human soldiers discuss folk remedies for the clap, his mind revved up into hysteria. He'd never felt so alone, so completely abandoned to the immediate, real panic of death. He hung onto his branch, fearing he'd piss his pants with fright. A fat leech plopped onto his cheek and dug into the skin, burning. But Meade didn't move. He'd been trained by the best. His fear still had no shape or logic to it. He couldn't think his way through it or out of it. It did not pass like malarial chill; it convulsed him. He was in the presence of death, with the peculiar smell it gave the body coming through the rotting cloth and mildewed canvas of his clothing and the fetid stench of the jungle. Death was an odor. It smelled of dried, salted fish and rice cakes that the VC four meters below his back were eating for breakfast. Death smelled of their gun oil, of their rubber Uncle Ho sandals, of garlic and bean curd. Any one of them could have spotted his broad, American back up in the tree and bayoneted him without getting up. The leech quietly sucked his cheek.

Suddenly one of the soldiers farted. A loud clear echoing burst of gas. The others laughed. Meade smiled to himself, suppressing a giggle. Good lord, he'd thought, I'm on the edge of torture and a hideous lonely death and I'm snickering like a college kid about a fart. And suddenly the fear fell from him like a coconut being split with a machete. Something snapped in his mind and Meade was alive with an awareness that he was the best. It came to him like a stab wound that he was born for this. He was very good at evading capture. That was the secret that the jungle held for him, that the soldiers below, bent on his capture, were forcing on him. To be invisible. That was nature's lesson for Meade. He was born for getting away, for passing through unseen. It was a strange power that held him then, an aura of confidence as gripping as a religion, more forceful than the knowledge of death.

His muscles relaxed. He ignored the leech on his face. He would win, he would get back to American troops somehow and make these VC trackers look foolish. He began to relish their closeness. All his life he'd been pursued: by family, military, the straight life. And now he'd found the answer. The more he was pursued, the closer adversaries came to him, the more he could elude them. It was his strength, his talent. Meade would make his mark by having no mark that anyone could discover.

The rain had let up in the Pinchot National Forest. Meade sat motionless against the boulder. It was almost full daylight now. He turned his attention to the campers' tent. A body was outlined against the nylon, then the flap was unzipped and a figure in a flannel shirt emerged on hands and knees. Meade sat quietly as the girl stood up. A very pretty girl of nineteen or so, and all she had on was a man's flannel shirt. Her legs were as long as a California freeway and beautiful. Her ass was simply amazing as it peeked whitely from below the shirttails. She stretched, her breasts rising under the shirt, and then she hopped on one leg and reached out for a tree limb propped against the tent. Using it as a crutch, she swung off into the trees behind the tent for a morning pee, Meade supposed. Maybe she had a sprained ankle. A tall, broom-thin boy with a blond ponytail, wearing only corduroy pants and showing off his scrawny chest, climbed out of the little tent and began gathering twigs for a fire. Meade began to croon quietly, "Hello young lovers, whoever you are . . ."

"It's a monkey's fist."
"What's that?" asked a perplexed Gruen.
Gulls screeched over Gruen's head on the pier of the Tacoma Salmon and Fishery Company. Willie Max, ex-coast guard and good friend, sat on a wooden crate examining the string Gruen had kept from the airplane. Willie had a face like an aerial photo of the Absorka Range of the Rockies; a craggy, elevated look as old and dangerous as a mountain. He was a gentle man, however, and Gruen's best pool-playing partner at the Soap Creek Tavern. Willie had a touch that could kiss a ball into a side pocket and stop dead on the spot. He had a subtlety

that took opponents by surprise, for they made the mistake of judging his barrel-shaped fisherman's chest and arms and his big rough hands as being an indication that there was muscle between the ears. It usually cost them ten dollars worth of nine-ball bets before they corrected the impression.

It was 8:00 A.M. and the last of the salmon fleet was on the way out, followed by clouds of gulls as avid and vocal as groupies chasing a guitarist.

"Willie, what the hell is a monkey's fist?"

"This knot is a monkey's fist, Bill, my boy."

"It's a sailor's knot, then?"

"Oh, in a way, but you wouldn't find many navy or coast guard men now who'd even recognize it these days. Today, kids have radar and remote firing controls and hair-length regulations to worry about. Maybe an old boatswain from the Boxer Rebellion might be able to tie it, but they're mostly in the old folks' homes now. Too goddamn old to skyjack a plane."

"Hey, Willie Max, I didn't say anything about—"

"You didn't have to, Bill. I'm not a dumb fuck, you know; not some old geezer hanging out on the pier." Indeed, Willie was dock manager of TS&F, Inc.

"What's that knot used for?"

"It ties off the end of a line so it won't unravel, and it makes something to anchor a line to when you're lashing up or tying off."

"If a sailor wouldn't know it, then give me your expert, old-geezer opinion as to what kind of man tied it." Gruen smiled at Willie, who could rarely resist in his quiet way to show his knowledge of the world. Willie could even get by in Chinese if he had to.

Willie scratched his craggy face. "Well, these stink fishermen around here that are out for Charlie the Tuna wouldn't know a monkey's fist from a skipjack. I'd say it would have to be a blue-water sailor, someone who loved the sea and probably has put in a lot of time under sail. That kind of knot is purely decorative now. It's like those damn brass eagles they put up over the doors of the new 'colonials' out in the suburbs. Pure show."

"So the guy who tied it is either a historian or a sailboat type."

"Yep. I'd think so. You be out to Soap Creek tonight for some nine-ball, Bill?" Willie got up, stretched his massive arms, and plodded back up the pier with Gruen, a huge paw on his shoulder.

"I don't think so, Willie Max. This skyjacking case is running my ass around pretty good."

"You think the guy who did it tied that knot, huh?"

Gruen stopped and leaned against the steel piping along the side of the pier, inhaling the brackish smell of low tide as small clouds scudded through the leaden sky.

"You have a few minutes, Willie Max?"

"Sure, the boats are out now."

"Everything points to my guy being a Vietnam Special Forces veteran. Now you throw me a curve about this knot."

Willie Max snorted and hawked a great load of spit into the ocean. "So? A Special Forces soldier couldn't be interested in sailing, too?"

"It's unlikely, you've got to admit. But there's more to it. When I got this bug up my ass about Special Forces, it made me feel a little strange, you know. This guy might be someone I trained, or fought with, in Vietnam. Christ, I may *know* the guy." Gruen watched a coot, one of those dumb, black, diving ducks, drop head first into the water and disappear beneath the surface. "Three of my men are sifting army records now, pulling every sheet that could be our guy—Special Forces, white, age twenty-one to forty, Vietnam service. You know how many there'll be?"

Willie Max shook his massive head in genuine concern.

"Two, maybe three, thousand. And we've got to eliminate everyone who's out of the country, got an alibi, or is already in slam." Gruen snorted, "Hell, some of 'em are even FBI agents."

"Maybe you'll get lucky. And, Bill," Willie Max beamed, "I read about the manhunt that's going on down by the border. Maybe they'll get this guy before he gets out of the woods, and we can play some hard-ass nine-ball tomorrow night."

"I wouldn't plan on it, Willie Max; whatever else we did in Special Forces, and God knows we did a whole lot, we trained those kids so well they can slip out of anything. And if this guy is as good as he seems to be, he's long gone already. I'd bet he's in Canada. Or he's gone to ground nearby. You watch, the FBI will diddle this one up. They've got a whole National Guard company down there now, and about all that will do is scare hell out of the deer."

Willie Max studied his friend. "You sure look all wound up about it, though. I think you're having a time of it."

"It's funny, Willie Max, but I've got the old itch again. If this guy *is* Special Forces, I want him. I don't want the FBI to have him, and they'll take eighteen months to do the job anyway, like Patty Hearst. I want him fast and hard and clean." Gruen slammed the edge of his hand down on the pier railing in rhythm to his words. "The juices are flowing again, Willie Max, my balls are clanging." Gruen smiled at his friend.

"That's always worth it, Bill. Just don't get 'em cut off."

They were dressed now, fussing with the campfire. Meade watched silently from the shelter of the trees. The kids had made no move toward the thick clump of cedar branches that concealed his Jeep. They seemed to be just a couple of crunchy-granola mystics dizzying around in the woods with a shit-load of fancy equipment. On the other hand, they didn't seem in any hurry to break camp. He would have to fix that. The sun had risen just above the tree line and hung like a tarnished medal in the sky.

It was odd, Meade thought, as the odor of the kids' brown rice reached him, how seriously the young can take themselves. He smiled when he remembered that morning standing at the window of his room in the Tokyo Hilton, watching the Ginza come alive with tiny figures scurrying to work and traffic jam the streets as a layer of thick pollution hovered in the air ten stories below his room. It was his R & R trip after he'd made it out of the jungle alone and fallen delirious and half-crazy into a Special Forces camp at the southern edge of the Highlands.

He'd stood there in Tokyo clutching the telegram from his father:

CONGRATS. ON COMMENDATION. PROUD OF YOU. ALL HERE FINE.

BRIGADIER RANDOLPH MEADE (RET.)

Meade threw the telegram in the wastebasket. On the chest of his tailored uniform was a Purple Heart and the Bronze Star. His escape had impressed the publicity-hungry Special Forces command. Here was a chance to show how awful the VC were, chasing this nice boy around in their country. It was a painful memory. Meade had unpinned the medals and tossed them into the wastebasket with the telegram. He'd ripped off the uniform, put on civvies, and gone out to the nearest bar. He'd stayed drunk for three days and then taxied out to Asian Military Command HQ, found the Special Forces colonel, and told him to stick the reenlistment up his ass.

Medals, awards, distinctions. That's what got people into trouble, he'd believed then. And maybe he still did. If a man wanted to be senator, president, boss, rock star, he was already in trouble. Strength was to be unremarkable; unknown, invisible. That was the secret the jungle held. In Cambodia he'd seen a tiger hit a spreading peacock. Death was a cloud of beautiful feathers. You had to be the color of sand and mud and trees. There was a secret power in the unobserved man, the one who could pass through a jungle, a city, a barroom, unseen.

He'd been foolish enough back then to make a speech to that effect to the Green Beret officer in Japan. It was Meade's last speech, half-hallucinatory from three days of saki. The colonel had merely thought him insane, another manifestation of combat fatigue. But the army had trained him well for his new belief. And it was time to test it now.

Meade rose and walked straight and loudly toward the campers' tent, where they hunkered, eating from stainless steel plates. Meade swung in on them empty-handed, smiling. No threatening moves here.

The dark-haired girl shaded her eyes. "Hi."

"Hello. You folks deer hunters?"

The boy laughed and dug his long fingers into his beard, as if searching for pieces of food.

The girl pouted at Meade, shaking her long locks. "We're not into that, you know? We want to get out of here before the slaughter starts, but I've twisted my ankle and it's all swollen, and Jeff thought we should wait until . . ."

Jeff smoothed his ponytail and quieted her with a

hand on her knee. He wasn't all that dumb, Meade thought. You don't go tell *everything* to some smiling asshole who walks into your camp. Kids had learned a lot from dealing in dope.

"I'm Jeff and this is Gail," he said, half-smiling at Meade, trying to keep his expression open. "What's your name?"

"Mason Roberts." Meade stuck out his hand and pumped Jeff's enthusiastically.

"You want some breakfast, Mason?"

Meade stuck his nose at the glutinous mound of brown rice burning on the bottom of the aluminum cooking pot. "Uh, no thanks, kids. I ate at my camp before I started out this morning. But I'd take a cup of coffee," he said nodding at their pot.

Gail smiled at Meade as if she were about to change a baby's diapers. "That's not coffee, it's herb tea. It's very energizing with honey and doesn't gunk up your system with caffeine and chemicals. They put lye in coffee, you know."

"They put it in bourbon, too," laughed Meade, "and coffee and bourbon keep America strong." Jeff laughed, too. "That's stupid," Gail said evenly.

After breakfast Meade told them that he was "pretty good" at first aid and taped Gail's sprained ankle from a small first-aid kit in their equipment. With his thigh pressed firmly against Gail's foot, Meade wrapped the tape expertly. Gail watched him with interest, looking for the insight that would break him open, the way a fighter looks for the opening that will down his opponent. And she almost found it.

"You don't look like a deer hunter. Or act like one, Mason."

Meade straightened up, half-amused. "Really? What do I look like, Gail?"

"I don't know. Your eyes are softer maybe. You don't look like the kind of person who'd shoot an animal. You don't even have a gun."

"To tell you the truth, I haven't shot anything larger than a bird since I was twelve and I left my rifle back at my camp." The lie came easily as part of his assumed identity. In one way it was true, if you didn't count men, Meade thought. He'd killed enough of those. "But I finally thought, you know, that if a man was going to eat meat, he ought to kill it himself, once in a while, to see how it tastes, how it feels."

Jeff looked up from where he was lacing the rolled-up tent to his pack. "We're almost vegetarians."

"Almost?" smiled Meade. Jeff fished into the pack and came up with a small foil pack called "Freeze-dried Beef Stroganoff."

"Is the deer I'm going to shoot going to be any less dead than the cow in the package?"

Gail protested, "But you *like* it. You want to kill."

"I never said that, kid." Meade wasn't happy about what he had to do now.

"Don't call me kid, it's chauvinistic. It's all part of the pattern that's ruining the country. Coffee, whiskey, killing animals. The whole country is crazy. That's what made Vietnam possible, so don't patronize me." Meade finished taping Gail's ankle, thinking of the purity of youth. Had he ever been that naive?

"Look—that tent you slept in last night? It's made of ripstop nylon. So's your pack and so's your coat. There's only one company that makes nylon. Dupont. They make napalm and a lot of awful chemicals that are polluting rivers and poisoning hot dogs and all that romantic load of dung. So you throw away all your fancy camping gear made by the killers and you go out and play girl scout with a sharp stick and a flour-sack dress, all right?"

Jeff laid a hand on Meade's arm. "Hey, it's okay, huh?"

Meade shrugged him off. "The world is a complicated place, and when you stand up and make speeches, you usually fall on your face."

Gail laced up her hiking boot and was able to hobble around pretty well. Meade helped Jeff repack their back sacks so that Gail would carry the lighter, bulkier items. He cut off the tails of his shirt and made them bright red headbands and arm bands.

"That should give most hunters a clue that you're not mule deer. Now, stay on the main trails and talk loudly and make noise. Dead environmentalists are tough and don't make good stroganoff."

Gail wouldn't give up. "Have fun at the slaughter, mister." Her little chin jutted out toward him.

"Relax," said Meade, "I'm not your father."

"Asshole." She turned and limped off down the path. Jeff raised his eyebrows and spread his hands. Meade nodded and waved. Like guests at a summer place, one thing that made people leave was a stupid argument and the one Meade had started was as stupid as any. Besides, it felt good to sound off at that smug little girl.

Before they were out of sight, bobbing down the fire trail, Meade heard a familiar loud clatter. Helicopter. So it was starting. The machine came over the ridge, olive drab, Air National Guard markings, dull sunlight glinting on its myopic bubble nose. He'd figured correctly. The authorities would overdo it, bring in the goddamn army. Along with the deer hunters and the locals, whose love of an easy dollar would bring them into the woods, it was going to turn the forest into a circus. And that was good, it would make getting out all that much easier in the confusion.

Meade walked into the middle of the fire trail as the helicopter clattered nearer, skimming over the trees, and he looked up, staring at it open-mouthed like any deer hunter who thought that the game warden was on the case. Small serious faces stared at him and the craft continued on toward the west. When its sound was gone, Meade began uncovering the Jeep.

2
THE WILDERNESS

Gruen saw a hunter gawking up at the helicopter in his orange cap. He must have seen a hundred of them today, and twice that many deer, leaping and lunging away from the noise of the machine. The craft tilted off to the west. There were two possibilities for a wise man in this situation, he thought. Either he'd have had accomplices and gotten out right after touching down, almost before the park rangers were notified, and well in advance of state police speeding toward the forest; or he'd have laid up. Laid up and what? Gruen thought as the machine swung over the highway outside the west end of the park and speeded toward the small town of Ariel, where the FBI and FAA and state police had set up a mobile command post.

If Carl Perkins was Special Forces, *and* followed his training, what he'd do would be to blend in, to become part of the scenery. He'd become a deer hunter. Gruen almost smacked his forehead against the Plexiglas as he reached for the radio.

"Wolverine three, to wolverine command."

"Go ahead, wolverine three," crackled the voice on the other end.

"Immediate alert. Have *all* deer hunters checked thoroughly, entering and leaving the park. I want a log of every person in and out of there. Detain anyone even close to the description. Out."

At the command post, a house trailer rented by the FBI and transported down to Ariel from Seattle, a dozen men in outdoor clothes with pistols clipped to their belts worked over maps, telephones, typewriters, and radios. It gave Gruen an odd feeling of his past—a military operation. The thick, blue automatic under his arm gave him an even more electric feeling. Until he remembered that they were after one man, not the whole NVA. He felt a bit ashamed of himself. Christ, there was enough firepower in just the command post to wipe out half the town. He turned his back to the activity and sat down at a desk reserved for him. He quietly removed the .45 and slid it into the drawer.

On top of the desk was a pile of one-sheet Department of the Army personnel records. There were close to a thousand of them, Gruen estimated. They were the computer-sifted "possibles" to match the description of Carl Perkins. Every white, five-foot-eleven-plus, twenty-five to forty-year-old blue-eyed man who'd served in Special Forces. When he was in the army, Gruen wondered how it managed to function in spite of its own repetitive, massive paperwork. But he regarded the stack in front of him without the weariness that had marked most of his two-year stay in the FAA since retirement from the Berets. There was something more immediate here; these papers probably contained his man. As he pulled the first sheet off the top of the pile, he fished the piece of butcher's string from his pocket and rubbed his thumb on the monkey's-fist knot for good luck. The goddamn thing was becoming a charm.

Three hours later Gruen leaned against the outside of the command post. He felt totally awake, energized. Everything looked more defined than usual; even the gray sky dazzled his eyes. It was like an R & R in Tokyo or Hong Kong after a month in the jungle. Across the street from the Sears parking lot where the FBI trailer was anchored, the Other End Tavern was doing a booming business, at four o'clock in the afternoon.

Even though state troopers had sealed off the roads into Ariel, it looked like half the wise guys in the state had sneaked in somehow. There were eight blocks to the simple main street, and all of them were parked solid with Jeeps, pickups, and station wagons full of gear and rifles. The sporting goods store cum post office that sold hunting licenses had a long line of men outside it, dressed for hunting, many of them drinking beer, joking, punching each other in the biceps. Many of them wore new boots and new shirts, bought hastily, Gruen guessed, to get out there after the two-legged deer that was carting $750,000 around in the Pinchot. The town looked like a frontier gold rush. All these dopes could run through the woods like the Chinese army. Gruen smiled to himself. What they didn't know was that Carl Perkins would run right with them. There was no chance of turning them all back. Even though the park was now ringed by a National Guard company, the border roads were long and winding. When he'd flown over in the helicopter, he'd seen vehicles swung off the road and their occupants already in the forest. A Jeep station wagon, its tall CB antenna bent with acceleration, roared past him, its occupants flung back against seats, beer spilling in a shower around them. A rebel yell yahooed from the window a lone, hunter's cry. Gruen hated to think of the "accidental" gunshot wounds that would be choking the local hospitals by tomorrow.

In the late afternoon gloom, Gruen took the string from his pocket, swinging the monkey's fist in front of his face. "Sailing, sailing, over the bounding . . ." It was like being struck by lightning. Gruen knew who Carl Perkins was. All the pieces fit. His body came up off the aluminum wall of the trailer on its own accord and before he knew that he was doing it, he was charging through the door, rifling through the piles of papers on his desk. And there he was, a small photo in the upper left-hand corner: MEADE, James Robert. Gruen slumped in his chair, smiling. He curled his huge hand around the monkey's fist. A knot within a knot.

The mule deer was a big buck, out early in the evening. He was stripping low larch branches with his soft lips. Once he put up his magnificent head, his wet, black nose twitching, as the light smoke issued from his nostrils in the evening chill. Then he turned back to his meal. His body, foreshortened and flat in the oval of the rifle scope, reminded Meade of one of those plaster deer people put on their lawns back east. The cross hairs of the scope stopped on his chest, just behind the front leg. Before he heard the clink of the shell casing hit the rock beside him, Meade saw the buck rise up a foot in the air, roll sideways, and land limply. His legs vibrated for a moment, the life running out of him, and then he was still.

"It was fast, anyway." He headed down the rise toward the dead animal, dreaming of the sea. Sailing was a dream that both haunted and comforted Meade in times of stress and action. Strangely he had not thought of it when he'd been chased through half the length of Vietnam. But as soon as he was in Tokyo, the sight of the flat Sea of Japan outside the window of his hotel, the calm luff of sails and the tilt of a sailing deck accompanied him everywhere.

Meade didn't learn to sail until he'd started playing with a Sunfish from a rental dock in San Francisco Bay, while waiting to be shipped out to Vietnam. Growing up in the Rockies, he'd read sea stories, learned the knots, played with model ships in the pond near the farm house, and dreamed of his own sloop. While other boys dreamed of the day they would have their own chain saw and log truck to imitate their daddies, Meade pursued his own fantasy. He was sailing a beautiful forty-foot sloop into Tahiti. It was made in Maine, fitted with the best brass and teak, immaculately white, its sails making perfect angles against the tropical sky. Brown girls with *National Geographic* breasts waved to him from shore.

Somehow dreams never seemed to aim at the same point as life. He'd ended up in the army, not the navy. The navy didn't have sailboats anyway, and although Meade considered it, he didn't wish to compromise his dream in a nuclear sub. He was twenty-two before he got his hands on the simple lines of a tiny teaching boat. He knew quite well what to do, and it wasn't long before he could make the little Sunfish stand on its head. After all those sea-less years in Montana, tying knots he'd learned in books, making diagrams of quarters of the wind and how to approach a dock, the reality of it was a jolt, a perfect one, and the little boy in Meade had rediscovered a dream, like a childhood sweetheart showing up in a strange city. When his fantasy had been touched by reality, it fired in Meade the desire for it to be a whole

life. To have a boat, a good one, and sail around the
world, stopping where he wanted, tarrying, loafing, the
slap of saltwater on the hull, living on fruit and fish
and whiskey.

It was time to bail out for good. And that took money.
And it even took shooting a big mammal like this deer;
a large, hot creature full of blood and sperm who merely
wanted to eat and leap and rut and smell the ozone after
a lightning storm; just about what Meade wanted for
himself. It just hadn't taken the deer thirty-one years to
know it and go after it. But there were scores to settle
first, the business of the world to elude or face, old accounts to close up.

Meade threw half hitches around the buck's rear feet
and ran the nylon parachute cord around his shoulders,
tying it off with sheepshank knots, so that he could
easily adjust the considerable weight of the animal to
drag it the half mile back to his Jeep. It was almost dark
when Meade started up the rise, leaning and straining
against the deer's weight, another burden he'd created
for himself.

It was almost midnight when the trooper walked into
the pool of yellow light behind the white, state-police
barricade, slender, tall, in a perfectly creased uniform,
and held up his hand for the Jeep to stop. Meade drew
to a halt, his body tense. This guy knew what he was
doing, he'd be a tougher adversary than those Sierra
Club kids. The pistol he wore was the largest Meade had
seen since Nam, a .44 magnum with a six-inch barrel,
so heavy it almost made the trooper limp as he approached the Jeep.

"Please get out of your vehicle, sir." The trooper stood a few paces away.

"Sure," crackled Mason Roberts of Walla Walla. "This some kind of conservation check? The deer's legal you know. See?" Meade walked up to the hood where the dead, gutted deer was lashed down to the fender, and pulled up the animal's ear, where the metal tag was threaded through.

The trooper pulled back another step and put his hand on the butt of his big handgun. "Please take your license and registration out of your wallet and hand them to me, sir."

As Meade did so, he realized that he was dealing with a competent professional. This guy wasn't about to answer any questions. Meade began playing a game with him, one he couldn't stop himself from doing, even though it was dangerous.

"What's the trouble here, Corporal?" he asked, looking at the two stripes on the trooper's sleeve. Let him know you're aware of rank.

"We're trying to establish identities, here," the trooper said, as he closely examined Meade's papers.

Ah, thought Meade, smart boy, laying out some good bureaucratic gobbledygook; he'll go on to a desk job, become an officer. "What kind of identity?" The trooper stared at him for longer than necessary. He's cool under pressure, thought Meade, trying to stare down my insolence. Meade let it work.

"Is this your correct address, Mr. Roberts? Twelve eighty-seven Olympic Street, Walla Walla?"

"Yep. Nothin' fancy."

"What's the zip code there, Mr. Roberts?"

"90778, Corporal. You gonna send me a ticket or something?" It was such a bum trick, Meade was no longer sure the young trooper would get to sergeant after all.

The trooper walked away to his patrol car, where a riot gun lay conspicuously on the hood. He pulled the microphone toward him and began to speak into it, holding up Meade's ID in the light.

Meade shivered against the night chill. The rain had stopped and now the cold was bone-aching. He zipped up his goose-down vest and wondered if it would work, the disguise which wasn't a disguise.

Meade had a three-day stubble of beard and he'd streaked his face lightly with dirt. He wore rimless eyeglasses and had the orange cap tilted back on his head. His too-big clothing draped over him, the pant legs piling up over the tops of his boots. He experienced a second of panic, that maybe the corporal would throw down the microphone and grab the riot gun and blow him away. Meade was unarmed, it would have been foolish to come roaring tear-ass out of the park with a uzi submachine gun blazing and crash the barricade. He wanted no alert sounded. He had to finesse this one. It gave him a secret pleasure to do so, and the panic released its grip on him. He could talk his way right through any goddamn wet-assed cop in the woods.

He looked at the Jeep. It was three years old, a little battered but unrusted. A roofing carpenter, a man who liked the outdoors and worked with his hands, wouldn't let a machine he owned fall into disrepair, even though he might not have enough money to get the dents knocked out of it.

The equipment and supplies in the Jeep had been carefully considered. There was enough food for a week, some of it opened and partially gone, enough to support his claim that he'd been out for three days. There were eight cartridges gone from the fifty-shell box of .30-.06 ammo. The rifle had been carefully cleaned after shooting the deer, like any good hunter would do. Along with a tent that he'd wetted down to make it damp, as if he had broken camp while it was still raining, Meade had stashed a half-empty bottle of Seagram's Seven and a dog-eared copy of *Penthouse* in with the Bisquick and cans of beans; after all, a young man off in the woods alone for a week needed a little private fun, huh?

The deer's eyes were open, where the head hung limply over the fender, moisture hanging in the long, girllike lashes; a reproach against this deception. Ah, don't stare, Meade told the deer silently, this is just like you used to do, standing stock-still in the woods, trying to blend in, trying not to be seen by the puma padding close by, and if he caught your scent, you could leap and run, forty miles an hour. I don't have that option, bud.

The trooper wrote on a clipboard and returned to stand a few feet from Meade. "I'm going to have to inspect your vehicle, Mr. Roberts," he said, handing Meade back his license and registration. Had he called up the reserves, Meade wondered, was this a stall? He thought for a moment of the broken down M-16 welded up under the rear drive shaft of the Jeep, so smeared with tar and road dust in its plastic wrapping that no wise guy would ever find it without taking the whole vehicle apart.

If the cavalry was coming, Meade wanted the goddamn gun in hand. But there would be no chance. He'd either blown it and it was down the tubes, or this uncommunicative trooper wasn't onto him. He knew that his identification would check out, he'd actually rented a place in Walla Walla, gotten a driver's license there, dressing for the picture on it close to how he was now. The Jeep was properly registered too, and Meade had only driven it once, up to the forest. There wasn't so much as a parking ticket out on it. The whole little play here, he thought with some pleasure, is whether this cop buys my story.

The trooper was thorough. It took him the better part

of an hour, and reinforcements hadn't arrived. Two more vehicles, another Jeep and a Blazer full of drunk Indians, had pulled up in line behind Meade's Jeep. A pair of National Guardsmen, cold and sleepy, had abandoned their posts down one of the park's peripheral roads to come to the ranger's shack at the entrance. They stood inside it, helmets off, drinking coffee and taking little interest in the trooper's activities.

The trooper had spread most of Meade's gear out beside the road, undoing tops of jars, unrolling the tent and sleeping bag, opening everything that could be opened. He'd used a mirror on a pole to check under the vehicle, carefully running it around the wheel wells. He'd felt inside the spare tire, felt under the dash. It was as good a job as United States Customs did at the Mexican border, Meade thought grimly.

"Hi-ya-yee-yee," chanted one of the drunk Indians, slipping out of the Blazer to piss in the bushes; the other men laughed and whooped. It was a hollow sound. The trooper looked distastefully at them. Meade thought that he didn't see noble redmen there. The trooper crooked his finger at Meade. "Help me get this deer off the hood, Mr. Roberts?"

"Sure. You wanna check that tag, Corporal?"

"No, sir. I want to look under the hood."

"You think this thing is stolen or something. What are you looking for anyway?"

"How long have you been out here, Mr. Roberts?"

"Three days, why?"

"You don't have a radio?"

"Nope. Why?"

The trooper didn't budge. "Did you talk to anyone out there?" he asked, nodding toward the blackness that was the wilderness behind the Jeep.

"Sure, some goddamn kids in an ATV roaring ass

around out there all fucked up. Probably dope. Say,"
Meade's eyes lit up in fake understanding, "I bet you're
lookin' for dope, huh? Heroin an' stuff? Sure, that's it,
that's all the cops do these days, huh, look for dope. I
never go near the stuff, I can tell you that."

The trooper looked away from Meade as if he were
very tired. He started to undo a knot in the nylon lashing
that held the deer strapped across the hood. He worked
at it silently for a moment. "What the hell kind of knot is
that?"

Meade kicked himself mentally for overlooking such
an obvious detail. He should have lashed the deer down
with a simple knot a carpenter would know, not a sailing
hitch. He wondered if anyone else would notice. He
would retie them in granny knots when he cleared the
roadblock. If he cleared the roadblock.

"Oh, I don't know, I just tie the damn things and hope
they hold," he cackled. He trotted back around the hood
and undid the other knot before the trooper could notice
that they were the same.

Meade grabbed the buck's hindquarters and the
trooper its shoulders. The trooper grunted as the heavy
rack of horns lolled over and slammed him in the chest.
"Son of a bitch," he swore, "he's a heavy fellow." They
laid him out in front of the Jeep. As he stood up, the
trooper noticed distastefully that some dark blood from
the deer's snout had stained his perfectly pressed gray
uniform shirt.

"Yep, he's a solid one all right," said Meade, looking
proudly at the gutted animal. "He must of been into the
orchards on the West slope outside the park. When they
eat apples they get well fatted up."

The trooper began under the hood, getting grease on
his hands and cuffs, checking the air cleaner and in between engine parts. Meade's heart rate went up to that of

a runner's. The son of a bitch was *not* going to find the money. He'd made it! But no celebrations, yet.

The trooper slammed the hood and wiped his hands on a rag. He put his broad-brimmed Smokey the Bear hat back on and fastened the chin strap. He helped Meade pick up his gear and arrange the deer across the hood. This time Meade tied him down with square knots.

"All right, Mr. Roberts, you can proceed. But be available for further questions in Walla Walla, we have your name and address."

"You still think I'm a dope smuggler?"

"Mr. Roberts, a skyjacker parachuted into these woods yesterday with $750,000. You don't think the National Guard would be out here for something routine, do you?"

"A skyjacker? No shit? That's a lot of money. I never saw anything like that in the park. I mean, you could have told me, couldn't you? Hell, you hold me up here for an hour, take my damn Jeep and my gear apart. Christ, what kind of deal is that?" Meade worked up a little helpless citizen's anger.

The trooper had already turned away from him and said over his shoulder, "Sorry for the inconvenience, sir." He'd forgotten Meade, he'd done his job and written down the right things and nobody could bust his ass for that. The trooper walked toward the Blazer, where one of the Indians had passed out over the hood, looking like a big deer.

Meade slowed six miles down the winding sloping road and pulled into a turnout next to the roaring, tumbling Mast River. He fished the bottle of Seven Crown out of the cardboard food box and sat on the running board, and took a great pull. He gasped at the rawness of the whiskey and smiled in the darkness. He was out of the park, no one knew who he was, and it would be a long time, if ever, before anyone found out that J. R. Meade—roustabout, North Slope Alaska oil worker, ranch hand, ex-Green Beret—was a skyjacker.

He took another drink and recapped it. With a big flashlight he walked to the hood of the Jeep and regarded the deer. A few black flies crawled around its head. Meade thrust his hand into the slit along its stomach. He tugged on the waterproof sack of money. It was there, slick with blood and gristle. He tucked it carefully back in, and listened to the dark river. The rush of water tugged at his thoughts; the white sloop was sailing slowly toward the shore of Tahiti and the girls in the bright skirts were waving to him.

Half an hour later, a speeding National Guard Jeep skidded to a stop at the east gate of Pinchot National Park. Washington State Police Corporal Arthur Lundquist read the FBI, WANTED FOR SKYJACKING, flyer carefully and stared hard at the photo of JAMES ROBERT MEADE in his green beret. He walked briskly to his car and picked up the microphone, a fine sweat breaking out on his forehead despite the coldness of the wind.

3
RUNNING

Cristobal, Sonora, Mexico, was as small and sleepy as a Gila monster dozing in the baking sun of the desert, but underneath its calm lay a current of violence and poison.

That, at least, was how Mason Remson saw it, looking from the dusty window of the adobe office on Cristobal's only street. It wasn't one of those picturesque Mexican towns where alcoholic writers came to die, or tourists used up a roll of Polaroid film, or even where some big-league mystic from Old Greenwich, Connecticut, would squat like a yogi and eat magic mushrooms. It was a plain, sad-ass desert supply center for the few hundred peasants who tried to get maize and beans to grow in the small mountain pockets of moisture at the edge of the baking plains.

Remson was skeletally slender; his sharp face to the window was battered West Virginia. His black hair was combed straight back and the bandito mustache he'd cultivated looked like a large joke on his thin face. He drank from a tumbler of yellow tequila and shuddered.

The goddamn town was shaped like a coffin, he thought, an adobe gate at each end of the street. At the backs of the shops the desert began abruptly. A rectangle where a disgruntled *Anglo* could scrape out a living, if he minded his business. Business was the Mason Remson Detective Agency, S.A. It sat next to the cantina, where a few indigent *brazerros* dozed drunkenly in the shade, and across from the market, where pathetic vegetables shrunk in the dry heat, and a lamb carcass hanging from the ceiling was black with flies. Next door was the mortician's. A dead infant swathed in white lace in a small coffin was propped up in the window, its blue-white, luminous, sleeping face pointed at Remson. The doctor's office had been closed for a year. He took another swallow of the tequila and turned away from the town.

On a cracked leather couch in the corner of the small, hot office, Mason Remson's whore lay with a wet rag over her face. Occasionally she dipped the cloth in a bowl of tepid water that sat on the floor. Next to the bowl was a tumbler of yellow tequila. Remson looked at her lumpy, splayed body in the cheap, flowered dress.

"Why don't you move once in a while and fix yourself up?"

She removed the cloth and looked at him, her puffy face marred by a small bruise on her cheekbone. "Why don't you go pull your prick, Mason?" she said in barely accented English.

He was about to say more, but the door of the office opened. A Mexican family stood there uncertainly, gazing around like they'd just won a trip to Mexico City. They were Mason Remson's corn and beans and he knew how to make them comfortable. In cracked Spanish he greeted them and drew up some straight-backed chairs in front of his desk. When they were seated, Remson asked, "How can I be of service?"

They were embarrassed. The husband, his straw hat in his hand and his big *cerveza* belly hanging over his work pants, slicked back his hair and looked at his wife, a portly, light-skinned woman with the fattest arms Remson had ever seen. She, in turn, glanced at their daughter, a sixteen-year-old with fine, upthrust breasts, and a face angular and clear. With tits like that, she'll go north for the line one day, Remson thought.

It was the daughter who spoke. "It is my brother, *señor*. Juan Carlos Miranda. He went over into the states last summer, and he has not contacted us since."

The mother rattled off a long-winded speech in the local dialect, something left over from Aztec and Mayan, which Remson could never understand, and produced a sepia four-by-five photo of some skinny, bug-eyed kid in a Mexican army uniform. It was always the same. Juan or Roberto swam the river into Texas and made it to L.A. or Phoenix and dropped drunkenly into the *barrio* after promising *mamacita* that he'd find work, and write home every week and send money, the fabulous dollars that awaited up north. Remson used a cheap detective agency in Los Angeles to locate the kids—half of them were in county jail anyway—and then he gave the family the info, for which they paid him an exorbitant fee that they could little afford. He had a reputation of not telling the law how their kids got into the United States, or that they didn't have the "green cards," work permits, or their whereabouts. The L.A. detective scared the shit out of the boys, telling them that if they didn't send a few bucks and a letter home every week, they'd be seeing United States Immigration for a friendly chat. And so Remson had become a hero in Sonora, and worried mommas and poppas came from villages and towns a hundred miles away on the hot, windowless, wheezing buses to enlist his services.

"My mother says that you are the best at finding our people in the USA, and she implores you to help us," said the daughter, sitting up straight in her chair, her breasts pointed at Remson.

"Oh, Jesus Christ, Remson, how can you live with yourself," hissed the whore, from under the cloth on her face.

Remson turned to her and drew his finger across his throat. He smiled at the girl. "You give me the details and tell your mother that I'll find the boy. I haven't lost one yet. Now, when did he cross over?"

The girl answered his questions while Remson wrote on a pad. "Now there is a question of expenses, here," Remson tapped the pencil against his sharp chin, his eyes flicking from the daughter's breasts to the father, who'd sat like a stone carving throughout the interview. And, as Remson suspected, he understood. He leaned sideways and drew from the tight pocket of his pants a wad of pesos. He glanced at his wife, who nodded, and he put the money carefully on Remson's desk. Remson began to count and from the way the family watched him, from the silence in the room, broken only by the slosh of water as the whore rinsed her face cloth, he knew that this was the family savings. Hell, he thought, they might as well give it to me, otherwise they'd just buy a goddamn television set and rot away. The money came to forty-eight dollars. Remson took a drink of tequila.

"Sometimes I don't know why I bother," he announced to the ceiling. Then he looked at the girl as if she were a puppy who'd just had an accident, and he spoke slowly. "You see this is forty-eight dollars, and that's hardly enough to start looking for your brother. It takes *mucho dinero*, you know?" Remson walked to the window and looked out on the baking street.

The whore raised up on her elbow, and said in mock-

Spanish accent, "What do you see out there, *señor*, Beeverleey Heels?"

"I think I know how I can help you." Remson walked behind the girl's chair and put his hand on her shoulder, ignoring the whore. "I am the best one to find your sons and brothers, huh?" The girl nodded.

"Well, it helps me a lot to know when the young men are crossing the border and who they are. That way, if there is any trouble, I have a start on where to look." He smiled confidently at the girl, staring down her blouse where the small gold cross nestled in the cleave of her breasts.

The girl explained in rapid Spanish to her father. It was bargain time. The father made a somber remark in dialect. He looked strangely at Remson.

"My father says that seven men from our village will cross on Saturday night. They have the *carta verde* for which they paid much money, but still they have to cross at night."

"I guess they'll go over the river at Big Bend, huh?" Remson said, apparently uninterested.

"Oh, no, sir," the girl replied proudly, "they are too smart for that. That is where the *federales* wait. They will cross at the lower bridge, where it is not expected."

After he'd seen them out of the office, Remson poured another glass of tequila and dialed a San Antonio number.

"Lieutenant Small, please." While he waited to be connected the whore shambled over to the desk, shaking out her black hair. She picked up the tequila glass and drained it in three big gulps. Remson reached out and drove his fingers between her legs straining her flowered dress. She moved away to the window.

"Small? It's Remson in Cristobal. I've got a load for you. Usual price, fifty dollars a head. Seven little Indians." There was a lot of talk on the other end.

"It's no skin off my ass if immigration doesn't want in on it. I won't argue price with you. That's better. Saturday night at the lower bridge. They're getting tricky, eh, Small?" Remson looked at the receiver.

"Son of a bitch hung up on me."

"You'd sell your mother, Remson." The whore turned from the window.

"So? You sold your ass all over this scorpion ranch until you got too fat and drunk to peddle it anymore. What the hell's your gripe? You think I got a white horse stashed in the barn? Well maybe I do, cunt."

"Not another scheme, Remson. I don't think I can take it."

"Then hit the bricks, because I've got a line that's going to get me out of this coffin town." On his desk was the FBI WANTED sheet on James Robert Meade. Remson picked it up and looked long and hard at the small photo of the tough young man in the green beret.

"One of my old army buddies is walking around somewhere with three quarters of a million on him. Shit, the insurance company is offering a twenty percent reward. But why bother with bringing him in?"

"Mason, they kicked you out of the army because you took shortcuts, you said. Is this another shortcut?"

"Well, well, another whore with a heart of gold. No, it's not a shortcut. He's a goddamn criminal wanted dead or alive. And I wasn't kicked out of the army, either. I was a victim of circumstances. Hell, everybody in Special Forces tortured prisoners. I just got tabbed by *The New York Times* is all. The colonel said he had no choice."

Remson drank deeply from the bottle of tequila. In the bottom of it a curled, dead worm floated slowly in the thin yellow fluid.

"I knew this Meade pretty good. A real loner, crazy cocksucker, too. He was good. Son of a bitch went it alone through the whole country. We got drunk together once. He told me about his old man and his wife in Montana. The guy had problems and he let his hair down.

"And after that he didn't even recognize me," Remson sneered. "It was like he was avoiding me because he told me about himself. So I've got no reason to love the bastard anyway. He might be good, but I'm no slouch, either. Just as soon as Lieutenant Small sends my traveling expenses from San Antonio, I think I'll just get up to Missoula, or wherever the hell it is, and have a chat with his missez."

The whore lay back down on the couch and covered her face with the cloth again. Remson walked over to stand above her, still holding the FBI rap sheet. "So how's about you say good-bye to me?" he smiled through a tequila haze. He lifted the hem of her dress and pulled it up. The whore didn't move.

"Is that you, Meade?" she asked. Distance crackled through the connection. She sounded tired. She often did when he called.

"No. It's Dialing for Dollars." He leaned against the wall of the booth. Just outside the jukebox throbbed some country song about heartache. You've really done it this time, he thought.

"This phone's probably tapped. The FBI is all over the place. We thought you were in Alaska this time."

"I'm coming home."

"Sure. Sure, you are." It was a statement she'd heard too often to be much impressed. And this time specially.

"You're just going to settle down and move back in here and putter around, huh? The town is like an armed camp, Meade. You can be such a shit, you know?"

Meade knew. "I want you with me. I'm coming to get you, Hannah."

"Look, I've got a business, Meade. Some stability here. Oh, damn. We can't talk about it on the phone."

"See you soon." Meade made it almost a question.

"I'll hold my breath." The line clicked dead. Meade stood for a moment grinning foolishly in the dark while the jukebox thrashed and wailed. Now it was some truck drivin' song. He remembered that the smart whores in Saigon had gotten onto the phrase "male chauvinist pig." But they couldn't say "chauvinist" in their squirrely English, so some soldiers were just known as "male pig." Those were guys who beat them or threw up in restaurants. Not exactly what a nice UCLA girl would think of these days. Maybe Hannah didn't think of him as a male chauvinist pig, but just as a pain in the ass. That's what happens, he thought, when you go out for a pack of cigarettes in Missoula, Montana, on a summer evening and call home a month later to say you're driving dynamite on the North Slope. You're a pain in the ass.

Meade opened the door and walked out of the booth into the main room of The Tin Horn Tavern and Restaurant in Hailey, Idaho. It was Friday, quitting time. The place was packed with paycheck cashers pouring down Olympia beer to take the edge off another week.

J. R. Meade was now a cowboy. The transformation had taken only an hour in a Western outfitting store in Eureka, Oregon. He wore Levis and Tony Lama boots; a wide, tooled-leather belt; and trophy buckle. Over a flowered shirt with pearl snaps he wore his goose-down vest inside out like a Montana cowboy, to show the label, so folks would know it was *real* goose down. Strange rites of the tribe. The Resistol hat was comically large, with a giant Tom Mix crown and a snakeskin band, but that's what these dudes wore.

Outside, angle-parked in the late sunshine, was a 1971 Ford pickup, yellow and smeared with mud along the rear fenders. In the back was a saddle and gear. Meade had left the Jeep in a junkyard in Spokane, where it would be a month before it was discovered under sheets of rusted metal, and he'd buried the deer. He'd picked up a set of Colorado plates from an old Dodge two-ton truck marked for the shredder. The pickup he bought, eight hundred dollars cash—cowboys still deal in cash—from a gas-station attendant several blocks away. By the time the law had it sorted out, he'd be on the way to Tahiti, the sails belling out across the blue water. And Hannah would be with him.

"Give me a cheeseburger, bartender." Meade felt suddenly hungry. The wiry little man with sparkling eyes and a string tie with a knuckle-size piece of turquoise on the slide, cracked, "I wouldn't get a cheeseburger, if I was you, cowboy."

"Why not?"

"The cook's down with the flu and all we have are those things." He jerked his thumb at a metal box that sat on the back bar along with Zippo lighter fluid, pickled eggs, Hav-a-hanks, Tums, a blurry photo of a group of bundled men holding up lake trout strings somewhere on a frozen lake, and an immense, stuffed steer's head. "X-ray burgers," he winked.

"What?"

"Well, they bring in these frozen sandwiches and then we're supposed to heat 'em up in that thing. They're already cooked. I tried one for the hell of it when they installed the machine. Pure shit, cowboy. I can heat up some chili for you. Our gal made that."

"Okay, cap, whatever's right." The bartender was called away by a loud group at the end of the bar; three young men in suits and stack-heel shoes, their hot-combed hair swinging fashionably in the rustic log building. Meade cranked around on his bar stool. A couple of ranch hands were playing pool. A group of sullen Indians stood at the shuffleboard, one of them wearing a black silk jacket that sported a colorful dragon and a map of Vietnam embroidered on the back and the name *Lonnie* in red. On the jukebox, Willie Nelson sang, "Take me away, Whiskey River," and two fat ladies at a table stomped their huge legs in time to it, shaking the pitcher of beer they shared.

By ten tonight, Meade thought, there'd be at least one fist fight, two incidents of adultery, and a lot of magnificent and useless whiskey talk. He wished he could hang around for it. A kind of farewell to what he would miss most out on his sloop. He wanted to drink with cowboys, fumble in the cab of the pickup truck with some young, bored wife while the fat moon lit up the pines on the bank of the Snake River. He wanted to have a fist fight in the parking lot, one of those swift, silent ones that brought you through the drinking into pain, and then back inside for more whiskey. Meade loved these hard, rough people. They were part of him and he would miss them dearly. They didn't have Waylon Jennings records in Tahiti. He made a mental note to pick up some tapes of the music.

The bartender returned with a huge, steaming bowl of chili and some Saltines. "This'll fix you up, son." The bartender looked at Meade for a long moment. "Where you headed? I haven't seen you around here before."

Meade's mouth was on fire from the chili. "Alberta, Manitoba. I hear there's work up there."

The bartender leaned over so that the metal tips of his string tie clanked on the side of Meade's glass. He whispered, "From what I hear, you don't need no work." The man kept his wink hidden from the room. He pulled his head to one side, gesturing with his baldness toward the now-familiar WANTED poster pasted up on the back-bar mirror next to an announcement for a church supper.

Meade felt the bottom drop from his stomach. He gripped the edge of the bar with one hand and smiled at the happy bartender. "There's a .357 magnum pointed right at your gut, bud. It'll blow a hole right through the bar, so quiet down," Meade lied.

The little man's face fell. He looked hurt. "Hey," he whispered in a raw voice, "I don't mean any harm. Hell, I didn't even know that you were him for sure. I just wanted to shake your hand is all."

Meade had been calculating the distance to his truck and the safety of the M-16, and how he could kill this man and get out alive, and had not heard the bartender's words. "What?" he snapped.

"I just wanted to say good luck." The man was grinning uncertainly.

Meade realized then that his reactions were too automatically army. His first thought was to kill this old fart. And he wanted no bloodshed. He certainly didn't want to hurt anyone innocent.

"Look, bud," Meade said, "I don't know who you think I am, but you're wrong. Get it?"

"Sure, Mister, I get it." The old man couldn't stop grinning. "But I just had to say that you really stopped the shit right where it ought to be."

"You've got to be careful," Meade said, relaxing slightly, but still whispering, "shit spreads."

"They've got shit up in Manitoba, too," whispered the old man, his face suddenly going dark with anger.

Meade wondered what he was doing sitting there with this old man who could blow the whistle on him the minute he was out of sight, talking about shit, the magic word that conveyed so much. He made a decision. He was going to have to disappear more conclusively. If every backwater, retired citizen recognized him regardless of disguises, Meade would simply have to get farther off the road, go farther back into the wilderness. The Tin Horn Tavern and Restaurant was Meade's farewell to American life for the present, maybe forever. It didn't make him happy.

By the time Meade had drained his beer glass, the old man had worked his way down the bar again. "Give me one more draft, pard, and then I'll be gone. I think I can trust you. I don't know why exactly, but if you cross me and maybe head for the telephone after I've left, we'll meet up again."

The old-timer didn't seem to be frightened. As if he were dealing with a friend instead of a wanted felon. "No problem there, fella. All you did was to set the bastards right. I think most of the folks in the country wouldn't mind pulling off what you did."

"Remember, I didn't do anything."

"Got ya." The old man served Meade the beer and moved off down the bar, called by the insistent voices of thirsty Friday folks. Meade sipped on the beer and began to work around the edge of the question that perplexed him.

The question was, How did the authorities stumble onto his identity? He'd left no fingerprints, nothing to identify himself. That he knew. The materials of the "bomb" were bought over the space of a year between Vancouver and Bakersfield, California, in large common stores. He had spoken only to the stewardess; there couldn't be a voiceprint. And no one, absolutely no one, could know what he had been planning. As far as his father and his Hannah were concerned, he was in Alaska, driving nitro and dynamite on the North Slope oil fields. But in the paper he'd bought that afternoon, there was his photo. How? He sipped the beer, cooling the chili fire in his stomach. The bartender turned down the jukebox from behind the bar and snapped on a huge color television set, hung from a platform high up behind the bar. Local news. The hubbub didn't die down for an instant in the bar, but people glanced up occasionally.

It had to be the stewardess, or the two kids in Pinchot. Something gave him away, and Meade was perplexed.

He'd figured on slipping out of the country unknown, down to Baja, where several sleepy boatyards didn't mind doing business with a man who paid in cash. Get Hannah, talk to the old man, and get out. Now it was going to be difficult. Meade smiled to himself. But difficult was what this game's all about. It would call for more planning, more care, more evasion.

Meade looked up and stared at his own face on the television screen. It was a shock. The smooth-cheeked Green Beret that stared back at him with such clear eyes, with such definite purpose, was someone he could barely remember. He tipped his hat down further over his eyes. Over the past hours he'd seen that photograph several times; under newspaper headlines and on several FBI posters in store windows. Apparently the Bureau was saturating the area with this picture of an earnest young man about to go destroy the enemies of his country.

As Meade prepared to leave the bar, a face filled the screen, replacing his own image. Meade stopped cold. His limbs went heavy. The face was Sergeant Bill Gruen. Meade shuddered in the smoke and noise and laughter of the Tin Horn Tavern and then began to smile. Sergeant Gruen. The best there was at tracking. They used to say that he could look at a VC bowel movement and figure out where the owner was and have him by nightfall. He was relentless and smart and tricky as hell. Now, the announcer was saying, he was some kind of FAA official.

But that didn't matter. He was still Sergeant Gruen. And now it was going to be a real chase. And a deadly one.

"You stay out of the shit now," the bright-eyed owner winked at Meade as he headed for the door. "If you walk straight across the pasture, you're bound to step in some cow flops, pard. You gotta learn broken field running." The little man laughed heartily, and Meade was out of the door before he stopped and began to wonder if it was Gruen who had figured out who did the job.

Missoula, Montana, sits in the crotch of the Clark Fork and the Bitterroot rivers. It is the home of the University of Montana, serves a wide area of consumers from the Idaho border to the west across to the continental divide in the east; a quiet American town of fifty thousand pickup-driving, tire-squealing, hunting-fishing folks who still have no posted speeds on their highways, pay negligible taxes, and pretty much operate as if they lived in the 1890s. And yet they are the most vocal people in the United States about individual rights and the ruination of the country. It is a town full of Grizzly Adamses posing as insurance salesmen and telephone linemen; it is half-home to hundreds of Flathead and Blackfeet Indians who make it into town to stun themselves on cheap bourbon at Eddie's Club and the Railroad Bar, only to be shoved onto buses Sunday morning to be sent sick and sweating back to Browning, Camas, and Polson. Missoula is not a big tourist spot, for, excepting the foothills of the Rockies rising to the south and the east, it looks like anyone's home. Sometimes worse than home. Like Los Angeles, Missoula has an air inversion pattern, which holds the thick, sour air from the town's several pulp mills close to the ground. There are days in Missoula when drivers have to switch on their lights to negotiate the yellow, fetid air. The affluent of Missoula live off in the hills outside of the pollution, where they can grouse and whine about the country's ruination without experiencing it in the least.

Like most American towns Missoula has a "strip," a stretch of highway on the business loop of Interstate 90 west of town—it is always west of town—where new businesses in their franchised architecture mushroom up to serve growing populations. McDonald's, Arthur Treacher's, Sears, Shakey's Pizza, a row of auto body shops, a Travel Lodge motel, a few drive-in banks, car dealerships, a disco bar or two. Everything shines and glitters there, all is new and clean. History is erased in the roar of the concrete trucks and the knock of a hundred hammers.

Bill Gruen sat on the new cement veranda in front of his Travel Lodge motel room as the sun blazed a last blast through the yellow air. He had moved out a sticklike chair from his room and sat with his feet up on the new aluminum railing made to look like New Orleans ironwork, watching the after-work traffic stream by on the Interstate. It was chilly and steam rose from the Styrofoam mug of coffee he held. He wore a sheepskin coat against the cold. The map of Missoula and the surrounding counties was spread out on his lap. He looked out at the traffic.

"Goddamn idiots," he muttered, but he wasn't thinking of the workers streaming home. He was thinking of the FBI. Several things had happened that enraged Gruen and would make his job extremely difficult. First, the FBI, in its rush to show the nation that it could identify a criminal, if not actually catch him, had released J. R. Meade's name and description over Gruen's strong objections. As usual the district director of the

FBI in Seattle had used the old argument, "It's better to have the whole country looking for this man, don't you think?" No, Gruen didn't think. The FBI still had some notion of the average American citizen as someone who spent the day peeking out of the front window noting license numbers of suspicious vehicles and calling the cops every time they saw a stranger. The Bureau was hopelessly out of it. But the main problem was Meade himself.

Gruen sipped coffee, the steam blowing up his nostrils, warming his aching sinuses. J. R. Meade was one of those army products so highly trained, so perfectly pitched toward the jobs of killing, tracking, and evasion, that it was frightening. Gruen had read accounts of Nam vets who went crazy and grabbed the old M-16 and started knocking off the home folks while checking the sky for helicopters. Meade wasn't one of those, but if the man knew the authorities were onto him, which he must by now, he'd not only be twice as difficult to find, but dangerous, too. Here was a man on whom very expensive training had been lavished. He spoke five languages passably well, could kill a man in ways that were ingenious and quick, could run—if he were still in shape, and Gruen guessed he was—all day. Could make his way through any wilderness, slip through guards and fences easier than a fox. He was a man who could throw bloodhounds off a scent, go to ground and live off the land for a month without surfacing. He could fly any military aircraft made, use exotic firearms with accuracy. But almost any Special Forces soldier could do those things. The thing that Meade did better than that—God knew Gruen didn't want him better—was that he enjoyed it. No, loved it. Meade loved the game.

Before Meade's escape from the VC he had been, Gruen remembered, a sullen, bright, young man, perplexed by his own excellence, defiant of any authority, one of those barracks-room lawyers who knew just how far he could bend the rules and irritate his superiors. He did his job of sapping the VC trails and supply caches like a master, but he was destined never to rise in the service. He was a perennial corporal.

But the escape from the enemy had transformed him. There was then, Gruen remembered, a new confidence in Meade. He no longer defied his superiors, he simply *acted* superior. Meade became the best jungle fighter Gruen had ever seen. The man had a natural ability and a belief in his own considerable powers. He was awesome. And that fact delighted Gruen in a strange way. Here he was in Montana, away from the hated desk, where everything melted into institutional gray and forms in triplicate. He was back in action, and he had a worthy adversary. Both of them knew the game of pursuit and evasion. It would be a chess game of military minds now.

The FBI didn't have a chance. They'd come through Missoula like a Marine invasion, taking depositions, opening mail, harassing everyone in sight, making a show in a small town that irritated and confused the local folks. It was typical of bureaucracy. Then suddenly, the FBI had decided that Meade wouldn't show up in his hometown, that he'd run for the border—any border —and had begun concentrating on airports, docks, and Canadian and Mexican details. They'd left the Great Falls field inspector with a handful of Washington-based agents and the rest had pulled out, leaving the town plastered with wanted posters and local news programs and newspapers full of feature articles and special reports on the background of America's most wanted man. In the local taverns and coffee shops old timers, and kids, too, for that matter, told their J. R. Meade stories to anyone who would listen—mostly each other.

Perhaps Gruen had been negligent, for he hadn't told the FBI everything he knew about Meade. Old Special Forces training said to hold back a little chunk of intelligence, keep something close to the vest. And he hadn't told them about the night in the NCO Club in Da Nang when Meade had gotten morosely drunk and sat at a table with Gruen and a few other noncoms and let his hair down. He'd told them about his father and his wife, about his childhood in Missoula. It was an ordinary enough tale, but in Meade's intense way, he had made it seem special, and it had stuck with Gruen, who as a master sergeant had heard a thousand confessions, a thousand personal histories recited. Gruen was dead certain that Meade would come back to Missoula before long, before he made any irretrievable move, if indeed he hadn't been there already. There were three weeks until Christmas. Gruen would stay at least that long. He finished his coffee, replaced the chair in his room, and got into the rented Dodge van parked in front of his motel. The usual FAA practice of using federal interagency motor-pool cars was self-defeating in this town. He swung out into the thinning stream of rush-hour traffic and headed west, down the river.

He had to consult the map only twice to thread his way through the dirt roads that snaked around the foothills down toward where the Clark Fork widened into a powerful, swift river. The sun was just dipping behind the pines on the butte across the river when he pulled the van into the camp. A hand-lettered sign nailed to the gate post of the slotted cattle guard separating the yard from a pasture behind it said, "River Trips, Inc., Raft and Power Boat, Day or Week."

Gruen was about to step from the van when a Siberian husky came cruising powerfully into view. Its pale blue wolf eyes stared at him. Its tail curled up on its back like a window shade. It didn't bark or pant. It sat down twenty feet from the van and stared. Gruen knew country ways well enough to know that you didn't get out and say "nice doggie." He did the correct thing. He honked the horn. It seemed to satisfy the dog, which lay down in the driveway, still pointed silently at Gruen's door.

No one appeared immediately. Across the river on a low butte, Gruen saw a man dressed in a hunter's red bib overall fire a high-powered rifle at an old lightbulb crate. He could see the crate jump and shred before he heard the shot. The man would adjust the telescope on the rifle after each shot; he was sighting in a new firearm. Everything about the man looked new from where Gruen sat. To fire the man leaned across the hood of what appeared to be a new Jeep station wagon. Even his clothing looked new.

Gruen honked the horn again. The man across the river heard it. His small figure turned in Gruen's direction. The man raised the rifle and swung it back and forth until the telescopic sight found him. Gruen's heart pounded. Son of a bitch, it's Meade.

The figure in red held the rifle on Gruen for a moment, and then turned back to the lightbulb crate. He fired and the cardboard exploded in long shreds. Hollow-point bullets, thought Gruen. But there was a fine sweat on his forehead. It could have been Meade, and *he* could have been a hunting accident. When Gruen looked around, a tall, pretty woman was standing next to the window of the truck, a businesslike expression on her face. The dog leaned against her leg.

"You look a little shook up, Mister," she said, brushing a lock of honey-colored hair out of her face. She smiled an open, honest smile, with a hint of an archness behind it. "The dog's not that frightening, is he?"

Gruen opened the door and stepped down, glancing at the hunter across the river, as a long crack of high-powered rifle came slapping across the water.

"No, I was thinking about the fella over there," he nodded toward the red-clad figure, "he's not real sure about where to point that elephant gun."

"Probably," said Hannah Clark Meade, "that's Woozy Horton—he's a dentist who just came to town from New Jersey, and he's not sure where to point anything, specially a .308 Weatherby."

She was a beautiful woman, Gruen thought, as he watched her amused expression. She reminded him of that stewardess. She was tall and slim but with generous hips filling out her Levis. Her hands were big. She wore cowboy boots, which brought her up to almost Gruen's six feet of height.

"What can I do for you?" she said. "River trips are over for the year. I shut the place down after Labor Day. I need that much time to work on the boats and the rafts and get some rest myself."

Gruen hated to identify himself. It was pleasant to stand out there by the roar of the river and talk with this woman. Gruen had not known what to expect of Meade's wife, but she was right, just right for that strange bastard. She looked honest and tough and would take no nonsense from anyone. You'd need that to survive a life with J. R. Meade. He sighed and pulled out his identity folder. "I'm Inspector William Gruen, FAA. It's about your husband." She took the folder from him and studied the photo, comparing it with his face.

"What the hell is the Federal Aviation Agency? Like the Civil Air Patrol? I can't keep all the agencies and bureaus straight. There's been a regular parade out here the past few days. I'm in the middle of patching a raft, come on in the boat shed and fire away." She turned abruptly and stalked off in a long-legged stride toward a log building behind the small, neat clapboard house on the river bank. The dog followed, silently. And so did Gruen.

Gruen held the orange rubber spread tightly over a smooth plank while Hannah roughed up the fabric around a hairline crack with a rasp and applied acrid-smelling rubber cement. "I told the FBI everything I know, which isn't much. Had to go into town and make a statement on tape and wait for it to be typed up and sign it, and swear I'd call them if he 'made contact' with me, all that stuff. Do you guys share the knowledge, or do I have to repeat the whole thing for you?"

"I read your statement, but it's a wild story. Meade went out for cigarettes one night last March and never came back?" Gruen watched her deft fingers.

"I found the truck at the airport."

"That's not unusual?"

"Not for Meade. He called a month later from Alaska. Up there driving dynamite to the oil fields. The time before that it was being a skydiving instructor in Phoenix, and there were runs of playing fisherman in there, too. He even tried to join the RCMP, but they wouldn't take him because he was an American citizen. He hung around Vancouver for a month that time."

"Was he like that before Vietnam?"

"I didn't know him very well before Vietnam."

"But you were married, weren't you?"

"Yes. But only for three months before he left for Special Forces training. I'd known him for years; we both grew up in these parts, but I never really knew what he was like, I guess. Here. Move this down now." Gruen shifted the raft material and spread out a new section over the plank, which she inspected as she talked.

"You see, Meade is one of those people who thinks he's

different from other folks. In fact he'll set around and think about how different he is for days."

"It sounds like you don't really think he is very different."

She wiped a strand of hair away from her face with her wrist; her hand was sticky with the rubber cement. She smiled at Gruen. "He's different all right. Look what he's gone and done now."

Gruen looked down at the orange raft. "Do you love him?"

"Hey, even the FBI didn't ask that." She cocked her head at Gruen. "Why do you ask?"

He wasn't sure. This woman was unsettling. And exciting. "I'm trying to find out if he'll come back here, is all. If he loves you, that increases the chances."

She threw down the patching kit and stood up, rubbing the small of her back with her fists, arching her back so that her breasts stood out, firm and round against the cloth of her flannel shirt. "Your name is . . . Gruen?" Gruen nodded. "Well, Gruen, he's told me he loved me for five years since he came home from Vietnam and during that time he's been around here only eight months. The rest of the time he's been diddling around in Canada and Alaska and points west. I suppose I love him. But you just can't live like that. He's been gone seven months this time and Woozy Horton and half the hotdogs from town have been out here trying to whisper in my ear. Someday, I'm going to listen to one of them."

"I doubt it," Gruen said with an embarrassing conviction.

"Oh, yeah? Well it might surprise you to know that you're a lousy judge of character. I was looking at you pretty closely, Gruen. You've got great shoulders. And I've got a hunch you were in the army. Am I right?"

"Yes. They've had my picture all over television, so

there's no reason to hide it from you. I was Meade's sergeant in Vietnam. I happen to work for the FAA now, and it's my job to tag him. I know what kind of man he is, I think, at least professionally. I trained him. And now I've got to get him. We'll see if I trained him *too* well."

"For your information," Hannah said quietly, "I love him, and I don't know what the hell he is, professionally or otherwise. If I ever see him again, I'm going to ask him what kind of man he is."

Gruen's heart went out to her; a tough woman alone. But then he was sentimental when it came to women. Maybe that's why he never married. When it came right down to it, he suspected that women thought him a fuzzy romantic. He had once killed a VC with a guitar string, severing his windpipe and carotid artery with one silent and powerful jerk. But around women he became courtly and stilted. They seemed to feel that he had a low reality factor, that he was too uneasy to truly like them. But an interview for information was something else, and Gruen's mind didn't allow his heart to interfere with that.

"Has he been in contact, by the way?"

Hannah turned away from him and began checking the supplies over the boathouse workbench. It was nearly dark outside and she lit a Coleman lantern, which threw a bright, hissing glow through the room. "No, he hasn't."

Gruen looked at her back. "Where can I get a steak around here? I'm starving. And you're lying."

She whirled around fire-eyed at him in the yellow intensity of the lantern light. Then she laughed. "Just down the road toward Lolo Pass is Tripp's. Mind if I come along? I've got my own money."

Mason Remson carefully fished a foreign object out of his mouthful of rice and beans. He got it onto his fingertips and examined it closely. It was a pubic hair. He looked quickly around, glaring at the few patrons in the restaurant. All were busy shoving spicy Mexican food into their mouths; no one paid the slightest attention to Remson.

The cook was Chinese. He was deftly curving tortillas and frying them crisp into taco shells over a big griddle. Remson slipped the pint of tequila out of his jacket and took a medium-sized tug, swilling the sour liquor around in his mouth like Lavoris.

Son of a bitch, he thought, I've come a thousand miles on a cramped bus full of drunk sailors and niggers and old ladies, all the time promising myself a good steak dinner, and I wind up in a Mexican joint getting some slant-eyed bastard's short hair in my beans. Remson pushed the plate away and sipped at the sticky-sweet Mexican chocolate. The Chinese cook stopped in front of him behind the counter.

"You all through?"

"Yeah. Great rations, there, fella."

"I can't eat Mexican food myself," the Chinese said, "it gives me terrible heartburn. I stick to bland stuff like cottage cheese, milk, soup, stuff like that."

"Sure. Listen, I bet there's been a lot of action in town what with J. R. Meade and the FBI and all, huh?"

The Chinese looked at Remson with a vague eye. "I guess so. Of course, anything looks like action here. I cooked in Reno for six years. Now that's action."

"Did you know this Meade fella?"

"I remembered him from the picture that was in the papers. He came in here once in a while. Most of these hicks, they only want Mexican food when they're drunk.

They're such pigs all they can taste is red peppers when
they're in the bag. I guess he was in here a few times
after the bars closed. He wasn't a regular or anything
like that."

"You think he'll come back to Missoula?"

The Chinese walked to the greasy window and looked
out on the street of Indian bars, two loan offices, and a
repossession center. "What the hell for? If a guy's smart
enough to jump out of a plane with three-quarters of a
million and not hurt anybody and get away clean as shit
through a goose, why in the name of reason would he
come back to this pop stand?"

"But I hear his wife and his dad live in town."

"His wife's got a good business on her own, and his
father is a fierce old bastard."

"I'll bet he comes back."

The Chinese looked skeptically at Remson. "You do,
huh? Well, everybody's got an opinion."

"Some are better than others."

"Probably, but if it was me, I sure as hell wouldn't
come back here." If it was you, thought Remson, you'd
just pull your prick in the beans. After he took care of
Mr. Meade, he was going to come back and wreck this
useless slope, too. That was a promise. Remson walked
out on the dark street, headed for The Railroad Board-
ing House next to the Great Northern tracks. The night
smelled of rain and a cold wind shafted through the wide,
deserted streets.

A broken-down M-16 consists of thirty-nine pieces.
Some of the springs and clips are so small they can get
lost in a crack in the floor. J. R. Meade sat with his back

against a tree, a poncho spread across his legs, where the rifle parts were spread out. He took a breath and closed his eyes tight. His fingers traveled over the parts, like a tailor's over a seam, fitting, assembling the gun by touch. It took him less than a minute, and as he slapped home a long clip in the completed piece, he opened his eyes in the darkness, threw the gun to his shoulders, and said, "Bang, bang, you're dead...."

Meade didn't know who was dead. He was sure he wanted no one dead. There was only that damned Gruen, and he shouldn't die. No one should. His mother shouldn't have died. Hannah's father, that kind and wise man, shouldn't have died. Meade didn't want to think about the bastards who should have died and were still walking around causing the world and themselves trouble. Many people, Meade smiled, remembering his father's phrase for army recruits, were as useless as tits on a boar hog.

He lowered the lightweight little rifle and looked out at the horizon. It was just getting dark; the sun had sunk behind the mountains at Lolo Pass to the west, leaving the fluffy clouds a pale egg yellow. "Red sky at night, sailor's delight. Red sky in the morning, sailors take warning." So went the old jingle about the weather he'd learned in Gloucester, Massachusetts.

A thousand feet below him the long, narrow valley spread out, the lights coming on the small towns of Last Dance and Perseverance, towns as strange as their names. Last Dance was a copper mining town that had played out years ago and now was home to a few Indians and a garage where the pop was always warm and a general store where Meade had bought supplies before he'd come up the mountains. Perseverance, a few miles down the road, was equally tiny, a town of Hutterites, German

Quakers who wore big beards and black clothing and whose farms, without expensive machinery, out-produced most of the ranches of Montana.

When Meade was a kid, a dozen young Blackfoot braves, all liquored up, had seized the general store in Perseverance, where the abstemious Hutterite owner had no compunction about selling Indians booze. The bucks had thrown out the owner, shot up the store, drunk everything they could hold, and when the state police arrived with shotguns and helmets two hours later, there was loud wailing from inside the building. Breaking in the cops found the Indians huddled on the floor with bolts of cloth, rifles, sacks of beans and flour, a wheel of cheese, shiny new axes, and a power saw. They were crying, tears running down their cheeks. One of them turned to a policeman and said, "Jesus Christ, we're rich. Please help us, oh, God, we're rich."

The story had haunted Meade for years, had been a touchstone in his memory. He had not understood it until that time in Vietnam. And then he'd handled its secret—people simply couldn't manage their dreams and desires. Accomplishment exhausted the imagination, and the simplicity of those Blackfoot braves shone through it. How many afternoons bucking hay or drinking in the sad bars of Dixon or Browning had they dreamed and bullshit their way through a dozen beers with the continuing soap opera of how they were going to knock over the Hutterite's store in Perseverance. A good name, Meade thought, a fairy-tale town. For to seize one's dreams took just that. And planning. Meade remembered when it had struck him that he was going to knock over an airline. Drunk in Tokyo in his hotel room. A foamy, drunk, Indian dream. But the next morning he began to mull it over, to work with it instead of play with it. It had taken six years to get it right, years of odd jobs, drifting, anything but perseverance if you looked at his life from the outside, but it had all come together. And Meade suffered no remorse, no panic, no end to the dream. They would be after him, the best ones the government could find, like Gruen, but he'd win.

The boat in Baja was no dream, either. And Meade didn't worry that when he'd set out, Hannah with him, crossing the Gulf of Mexico, white sails taut in the wind, he'd suffer an instant of doubt. This was his life and he was going to leave the bastards something to remember. Those Indians had done three years of hard labor in Deer Lodge state prison and were considered lucky. When they got out and went home, the Hutterite who owned the store sold them whiskey without comment, without judgment perhaps. One brave committed suicide. Not unusual on the reservation. Two went to Minneapolis to work as welders, a trade they'd learned in prison, and the others . . . he didn't know. On the reservation probably, picking up odd jobs, eating beans with fat wives, fist fights on Saturday nights. He wondered if they'd learned about the nature of daydreams, if they ever thought back on themselves, sitting on the floor of that store, surrounded by goods, a fortune they could no more handle than they could become part of the American dream. Details. What the hell was that Indian going to do with the power saw? His shack on the reservation couldn't possibly have electricity.

The valley was in darkness now; aside from the two towns below, Meade could see only the spreading black floor of it. Beyond the next ridge of mountains was Missoula and Hannah. And his father. Meade had set up a small camp on Darling Creek, a blue-ribbon trout stream that gurgled down the mountainside into a small lake. He was dressed in waders, a hat with trout flies stuck in the fleece band around the crown, and old

clothes. He had a tent and the usual camping para-
phernalia; all of it had been stashed here months ago.
He had similar rigs that had been buried in waterproof
bags all the way from Lake Louise in Canada to the
Grand Canyon stretch of the Colorado.

And that, thought Meade, was what was wrong with
most so-called crime, like those damn Indians. No planning. He threw a chunk of fat pine on the small campfire near the tent. The weather was colder now, biting
down below freezing some nights, but the streams were
unfrozen and fishing deep with wet flies was a prime
pastime for Montana trout fishermen. He was not unusual out here, not out of place. Any law officer wouldn't
look twice. Meade had bundled himself into layers of
clothing which both protected him from the weather and
gave him a stocky look that didn't jibe with the FBI
description. And more planning was necessary now: how
to get into Hannah's and the old man's when the FBI
knew he might be coming. He'd called Hannah, and he
knew she'd keep quiet about it. If the FBI had tapped
her phone, that was all right too. There wasn't a day
when Meade didn't feel he could outwit the slow and
grinding machinery of the Bureau. And probably Hannah had had too many of those "I'm coming home to get
you and take me with you" phone calls: from Gloucester,
Calgary, Prudohe Bay. This time it would be a surprise.
He leaned back and drew the goose-down coat tighter
around his shoulders in the cold, warming his face with
the tin cup of hot coffee. This time was a lot different.

Gruen stood before the knotty-pine bookshelves in
Hannah Meade's living room, running his eyes over the
titles. *Piloting, Seamanship and Small Boat Handling*;

Bowditch's *Navigation; Power Squadron Safety Book.*
They must be Meade's, he thought. They were old
editions, well worn. He had a mental picture of a teen-
aged boy sitting in his bedroom looking out at the endless mountains and valleys and dreaming of the sea, a
book of tide charts open on his lap. *Moby Dick,* a few
volumes of Conrad. *The Old Salt's Book of Knots.* Gruen
was amused. He took out the slim volume and flipped
the pages. Under a diagram of the monkey's fist, he read,
"A decorative knot used to secure the ends of small lines.
No knot can say more about your knowledge of tall ships
than the monkey's fist. One of the most difficult to tie.
Follow the directions slowly and don't be discouraged.
It will take a few attempts to get it right."

Gruen took out his key ring. He'd looped the piece
of string on it, and the monkey's fist that Meade had tied
on the airplane swung there. It was the final clue that
had tipped Gruen to Meade. The description in the book
was much like the problem in life—the most difficult to
tie, and the most difficult to unravel, too.

Hannah brought two mugs of black coffee. She handed
one to Gruen and sat down in an old armchair. The
steak down the road had been surprisingly excellent, for
a place called Tripp's Truck Palace. They had the best
hashed brown potatoes that Gruen had ever tasted. In the
bright glare of the place, with the clashing of dishes from
the kitchen and the loud conversation of a dozen truck
drivers and the boom of the jukebox, Gruen and Hannah
had no chance for conversation. Gruen had noticed that
she ate heartily, sopping up her steak juices with a piece
of bread. She looked at peace with herself and regarded
Gruen with what he thought was some amusement, the
way one looks at an old dog who's made a mistake and
demanded to be let out of the house through a closet
door.

"These are Meade's books?" He waved his mug at the collection.

"Yes. Although you know he didn't so much read them as fondle them. Sometimes I'd notice one or two gone when he took off to Canada or Gloucester. He's got a thing about sailing." She sipped her coffee and then set it on the table beside her. "I'd like to see how good you are, Sergeant. Take a look at the books on the other side of the fireplace and tell me who they belong to."

"I'm not a sergeant any longer, ah, Mrs. Meade."

"We just ate dinner together, call me Hannah. And you army guys, you Special Forces guys, are always army. It doesn't matter if you retire or quit like Meade."

Gruen sipped at his coffee, disturbed by her comments. If she thought of him as her husband's pursuer, someone who would willingly slap his ass in the clink and throw away the key, why did she have dinner with him? And if she didn't dislike him or what he represented, what did that say about her relationship to Meade?

He walked to the bookcase on the opposite side of the wide hearth and gazed at the fat, dark, bindings, *Ring Acceleration Theory, Advanced Thermodynamics Core Fission in Breeder Strata,* and *Matching the Hatch, The Atlantic Salmon,* and piles of *Fly Fisherman* magazine.

"Well, Sherlock," Hannah smiled, "whose books are those?"

Gruen was tiring of the game. His mind was only focused on Meade—anything else seemed to mentally exhaust him, he'd noticed. He was irritated by that fact. "Well, they're not yours, that's for sure."

Hannah became serious in a clear, unemotional way. "They are my father's books. He died last year of a heart attack." She stood close to Gruen, as if they were examining an old master. "I inherited his business. The books are arranged in the way he lived his life. My old man was a physicist at the Princeton Institute." Gruen noticed that all of those volumes were by the same author—Dr. Eric Clark. Hannah Clark Meade, from the colorless FBI report.

"He was one of the big timers, too. When I was a kid, helicopters would land on the Institute lawn and fly him off for an afternoon in Washington. Or he'd ride the train up to New York for a consulting job." She wandered back to her easy chair, letting her fingertips graze over the old and familiar objects in the room, as if summoning the past. Gruen walked over and sat on the couch opposite her, listening. Any tidbit could be the key to unlocking Meade.

"He wasn't one of those fuzzy-headed think-tank types, either. He was a big guy who bought tailor-made shirts and loved cocktail parties and good tennis." She giggled. "He once punched out the chairman of the English department when they'd both been drinking."

"But he was more than that, wasn't he, Hannah?"

She looked sharply at Gruen. "Yeah, he was more than that, Sergeant. You know, you remind me of Meade quite a lot."

"How so?"

"You listen well. You lead a person through a story, trying to make them see things in it. In themselves. Meade does that . . . did that.

"Anyway, my old man had a long, drawn-out fight with all the nuclear energy people; he was on the committee to ban weapons and power plants and all. Finally he was just disgusted. He came out of his study and said to me one day, 'Well, kid, let's go fishing.' And we moved out here and he started the raft business just to look respectable, I think. He had enough money salted away for the two of us for years. He never talked about physics or nuclear energy after that. We lived here like mountain folks."

"And your mother . . . ?"

"She died when I was seven. From then on I was with my father."

"How did you meet Meade?" Gruen wanted to keep her on the track. For his own sake. He was beginning to be fascinated with this woman's story. There was a great deal of strength and intelligence here. Keep her mind on Meade. That was interrogation. And keep your own mind on Meade, he reminded himself, looking away from the form of the woman in the tight Levis.

"It was all tied in together. This old son of a bitch of an ex-general came over one day, just a month after my dad had started the raft trips. Acted like he was doing us a favor. His son, who was Meade, came with him, the most silent kid I ever met. He'd watch his father, then he'd watch my father. Like it was some kind of test. Meade and I had a lot of father stuff going. Meade's mother had died when he was young, too. And his old man, when you first met him, acted like the Big West Wind from East Sweet Jesus. My dad was a pussycat by comparison. Meade was a silent kid then, with eyes that were too old for him, always watching, listening. I was a blabbermouth and anyone silent was fascinating. He was fourteen at the time; I was a year older. I would have walked across the water for him right then and there. It's been mostly the same since."

Whatever had been lurking in the back of Gruen's mind about Hannah suddenly disappeared. Her declaration of love for Meade had shut down his revving libido. He returned to business with a sigh.

"If your old man was such an important physicist, he must have had some security around him; FBI, and so on."

"That's the ironic part, Sergeant. Of course the FBI kept tabs on my father when he was at Princeton, but we didn't hear from them out here in Montana. My dad often said he expected some agent dressed up like a cowboy but wearing a snap-brim hat to start hanging around the place, but they never did. And then we found out why. It was Meade's old man. The Brigadier."

"He was the surveillance?"

"Yup. It came out after we'd all gotten to know each other on that raft trip. He had just retired and the FBI had come to him and told him they'd appreciate it if he kept tabs on Professor Clark for them."

"He *told* you that?" Gruen was amazed. "He shouldn't have."

"Relax, Sergeant. The Brigadier had no reason to love the government. More coffee?" She stood up, stretching her long body, and it sent a pang through Gruen. He followed her into the pine-paneled kitchen while she refilled their cups. Outside he could see the silent husky sitting in the shadows made by the powerful yardlight.

Hannah handed Gruen his mug of coffee. "My dad and the Brigadier. Neither of them loved the government so much by that time. They had a kind of bond that way, even if they were opposite personally." She smiled, a wide, genuine delight. "And besides, the Brigadier could see that my dad wasn't about to contact the Russian submarine that lurks in the Clark Fork River."

"Did Meade know about all this?"

"Of course. I blabbed everything to him. He could be very dumb about the ways of the world. Until after Vietnam. He changed over there. Now he can read people like the funny papers."

Gruen glanced at his watch. It was late and he wanted to get back to his motel and call Washington. He wanted the FBI files on Professor Clark and Brigadier Meade.

He could have them in the Missoula field office by morning. He set down his mug of coffee.

"It's late, Hannah, and I've got work to do, tonight. But I want to talk to you more. Are you free tomorrow?" Gruen realized that once she'd had a chance to think all this over, she might clam up. It was possible that she was in contact with Meade. He was sure she'd been lying earlier in the afternoon when she'd answered that question. And if Meade knew that Gruen was questioning her, he'd tell her to shut up, or knowing Meade, to get him off the track somehow.

But the real reason, Gruen saw, was that he was very attracted to this intelligent, lovely woman. If he stayed here longer, he was going to do something that he hadn't done in quite a while—put the make on her. When he thought about it, there were a lot of things he hadn't done in a long time. He was alive again, into the chase. A skyjacker, a woman, his own sense of adventure. Gruen was back in action. But he wasn't quite ready for this woman. When the affair with Meade was settled, maybe.

"Hey, Gruen," Hannah spoke quietly, as he headed for the door. "You're as dumb as Meade, you know it?"

"What?"

"Here I've been trying to seduce you all night, and you just keep asking questions." She turned away from him and began rinsing the coffee mugs in the sink. "Oh, don't pay any attention. I just haven't been attracted to anyone since, well, it's been a long time. And you're so goddamn silent. Another wooden Indian. Maybe I go for anybody who'll just stand there and listen."

Gruen moved near her and put his hand on her back. "I don't think so," he said with sincerity.

When she turned to him she was smiling widely. "Don't be so frigging serious." Gruen bent and kissed her. When he released her he could read nothing in her eyes.

Outside in the chilly wind, confused and alive with possibilities, Gruen had the distinct impression that Meade was very near. He felt it surely—Meade was going to come to Missoula, and he was going to be right there to greet him.

4
THE BRIGADIER

Meade crawled through the wheat on all fours. Above him the stars were thrown against the ink-black sky like drops of phosphorus. The half-frozen field hurt his knees and stubble poked into his gloves. He knew the field perfectly and avoided a low spot where gathered puddles were coated with water-thin sheets of ice, and headed purposefully toward the rise at the edge, over which he'd be able to observe the farmhouse and its outbuildings before he went down to it through a broken line of trees that offered some cover. If he went down to it at all. The moon was a sliver on the horizon above the mountains. The night was not bright, but there was enough light for Meade to make his way without a flashlight. The only weapon he carried was the survival knife. And he knew what was going to come through the wheat soon. He took the knife from its scabbard and held it loosely as he crawled.

Within a minute he heard it. A long scuffling in the

wheat, the whisper of grain stalks against fur, the ragged breathing. He raised his head to see the wheat twenty meters away parting in a waving line. He could feel the animal's power shake the hard ground as it drove toward him. He sat back on his butt, holding the knife low and pointed up by his side, ready to take the velocity of the charge.

The Siberian husky was immense for its breed. It weighed 115 pounds; purposeful, intelligent, fine-tuned to attack anything within the perimeter of its training. It broke through the curtain of wheat ten feet from Meade, slowing an instant to observe him, its blue, wolf-eyes bright, and its great ruff of silver neck fur framing the open jaws, the long teeth reflecting the starlight. It shifted back on its haunches for one final leap at Meade.

"Starboard! Starboard!" he hissed, gripping the knife firmly.

The dog, looking confused, flopped immediately down in the wheat, slamming its chin into the dirt, unmoving, as if Meade's command had killed it. And then the animal took in Meade's scent and it began to whine, straightening its curled tail in a sweeping motion along the ground.

"Good boy, good boy," Meade whispered, smiling. "I'm glad the Brigadier didn't change our commands, Mike, or we'd have to do some wrestling, huh?" He sheathed the survival knife and slowly reached to pat the dog's wide, thickly furred head. The animal whimpered and panted.

When Meade was ready to move again, he whispered to the dog, "Port!" and the animal, with a shake of its coat, trotted off into the wheat as Meade worked along toward the edge of the rise.

There were three of the huskies. One more down with the Brigadier and one with Hannah. Meade had trained them after he'd returned from Vietnam. The Brigadier knew the correct procedures for training guard and attack dogs, ways that didn't involve the brutality that quicker methods required. And it had given Meade immense pleasure in his favorite game of evasion to work against the half-trained puppies as they sniffed him out over the two hundred acres of the farm and buildings. The commands "port" and "starboard" were Meade's. And he'd sealed the dogs' loyalty to Hannah and the Brigadier before he'd left for Alaska. They were the only two people aside from himself who knew the commands. And · Meade was relieved that no one had seen fit to change the commands, a difficult and time-consuming task even for him. The dogs had been some kind of gift to the two people he cared for, an apology for his absences, maybe trying to make up for what he was going to do.

For when Meade had left for Alaska, he'd already planned the skyjacking and the escape to Mexico. He'd wanted to establish his pattern of taking off whenever his roving heart needed to, and Alaska was the perfect place. At the time he hadn't dreamed that the authorities would have tumbled to his identity so quickly, and he was pleased to see that the added planning, although not necessary, had been correct. Communications in Alaska were not the best. There were times on the North Slope when all communications died in the minus-forty-degree weather; only one radio was kept open for emergencies. And since neither Hannah nor the Brigadier knew exactly where he was, or how to reach him, he thought it as good a cover as any. And also it was easy to pick a target for the skyjacking from the top of the world, following out longitude lines from this source. He hoped that his didn't look like the kind of planned life that could handle a well-executed crime. But they'd tumbled to him and now the pursuit would be relentless. There were no chances for slip-ups.

Meade reached the edge of the wheat field, where the grain died off into stubbly vetch. He worked his way out into the open, flat to the ground in an infantryman's crawl, and worked to the edge of the small rise. The scene below, so familiar, called up in Meade a stream of memories, so that he enjoyed it for a long moment without worrying about cover or observers.

The farmhouse, severely white and unadorned Victorian, stood square with the sides of the valley. The windows were tall and glowed with yellow light. The lawn, close-cropped like a military haircut, lay around the house, transsected at points by straight gravel paths. There was a long, three-car garage, a barn, two sheds, and a small building behind which a large cement pad was broken up by chain-link, fenced-in dog runs. There were twenty dog pens. The whole farm made Meade grin. It said "army" in capital letters. The outbuildings stood as square and straight as noncoms saluting the house, a staff-rank officer, rising over the valley.

Meade saw lights come on in the big garage and could make out the whine of a power tool through the clear, thin air. To his right a windbreak of pine trees marched down to the edge of the first shed on Meade's side. He scanned the farm carefully, looking for anything out of place, satisfied that if anyone awaited him except the Brigadier and Billy Sky, he had to be a thorough professional. Meade worked to his right, rose into a crouch, and ran tree by tree down the hill.

Inside the big, heated garage Brigadier Randolph Meade (Ret.) held the woodworking chisel against the length of cherrywood screwed into the lathe, working from the model before him. Thin curls of the reddish wood gathered at his feet as he deftly shaped a Sheridan-style table leg. Behind him, the garage held several vehicles, all backed in, ready to go on a moment's notice, like an army-base motor pool. There was the Brigadier's silver Continental; a covered Jeep with power winch, radio, and extra gas tanks and spare tires; and a van, bearing the legend on the door, "Upland Kennels—AKC English Pointers—Hunting Dogs Trained." On the walls shelves and sheets of pegboard held the tools of a cabinet-maker in orderly rows. The garage was spotless. Beneath the oil plug of each car was a drip pan.

Near the Brigadier's leg a husky dozed on its side, occasionally clicking its black claws against the concrete in some dream of pursuit, beneath the whine of the lathe.

The Brigadier was a straight and slim six feet four inches, his short hair as neat as his farm. He wore a blue wool shirt and green whipcord trousers. His gleaming jodhpur boots were polished daily by Billy Sky, an old Flathead Indian who helped out and was the best dog trainer the Brigadier had ever seen. The Brigadier's usually hard face softened as he worked on the wood, shaping it, bending it to his wish, almost like working with men in the army.

He was an intelligent and devoted man, a rare combination that often tormented his sense of duty. His face was healthily tanned but there was a sunken quality to his blue eyes that stared out over the high, smooth cheekbones. There was a small bit of toilet paper on his sharp chin where he'd cut himself shaving.

When he'd finished roughing out the leg on the lathe, he turned off the machine and unscrewed the wood. He took it over to a workbench where an unfinished, glowing-grained handmade reproduction of a Sheridan coffee table rested. The newel post of the leg slipped firmly and perfectly into the hole on the bottom side of the table under the guidance of the Brigadier's gentle pressure.

When the husky rose with a groan and began pacing the garage silently, its tail curled like a rattlesnake, the Brigadier was not surprised. And when he heard the muffled "starboard" from outside the side garage door, he sighed aloud.

The dog flopped down tight on the concrete. The Brigadier opened the door and stood looking at his son.

"Come in out of the cold, J. R. That beard looks like hell. But then I guess you've got to hide your face." Meade's scraggly, two-week-old beard didn't cover the awkwardness that he usually felt in his father's presence. He slipped into the garage as the husky, catching his voice, began thumping its tail.

"You were expecting me?"

"Let's say I'm not surprised. Hannah came over yesterday to say you'd called. She thought you were full of it as usual, but she doesn't know your problems the way I do."

"I don't know," Meade said evenly. If the old bastard expected him to bow and scrape he had another thought coming. "I've got lots of problems." Best take it easy and see how the old boy was setting.

"I must say though, even I didn't think you'd go this far. I've already told the FBI that I'd contact them if you showed up or called. I almost phoned Great Falls yesterday after Hannah stopped by. I think I should have." The Brigadier went to the workbench and removed the newly shaped leg from its socket. He slapped it into his palm as if it were a swagger stick.

"Why didn't you?" Meade knew that they both needed some declaration, or defiance, or battle to settle this. He realized that he was probably seeing his father for the last time. Meade was going sailing and his father would be seventy in the spring.

"Why in Christ's name did you go pull an awful stunt like that?" The Brigadier slapped the leg in his hand with a sharp, painful sound. He was using the old counter-question technique that staff officers favored, Meade grinned inwardly.

"It wasn't awful, General," Meade mocked in semi-military talk, "it went as planned. No casualties and objective accomplished, just like you and the U.S. Army taught me so perfectly."

The Brigadier raised the table leg as if he were about to threaten a puppy that had peed on the carpet, "Don't be a smartass now, J. R. You're in the sling. I tried to sound out the FBI people about a deal if you returned the money. They weren't interested. They're going to have you for breakfast when they catch you. It would have killed your mother."

"Don't bring that up, General." *General* was what Meade had called his father since the man had made the rank before Meade had gone to Vietnam. When Meade could first talk, it had been *Lieutenant.* With each war and each new base where he'd gone to school, the name of his father had changed. "My mother's heart was broken by gin." The Brigadier glared, and then seemed to sag.

"Come up to the house." The Brigadier picked up a piece of emery cloth and a bottle of lemon oil from the bench and stalked from the door.

As Meade came out of the garage door, he saw the figure by the wall a moment too late. He heard the hammers of the shotgun click back. Meade rolled quickly away from the sound, his shoulder and back biting into the ground, heard his father yell, "No!" and then he bounded up, the knife in his fingertips, ready to throw it and run.

"J. R., don't!" The Brigadier's voice had lost none of its military authority. Meade paused, unsure. The figure with the shotgun was a rumpled mass of thick clothes that smelled of kerosene. The hammers of the old .10-gauge sawed-off cannon clicked down slowly. Billy Sky grinned his weathered, white-tooth smile at Meade.

" 'Lo, Junior. Sorry I scared you. I heard you might be back. I didn't want nothin' to happen to the General. Or you either." Billy Sky's pot belly was as hard as a rock. Presently it was full of Tokay, as were his eyes. But even paralyzed drunk Billy Sky was a formidable opponent. He could have torn Meade to pieces with that huge elephant gun. The cold wind came howling through the dark. Meade shivered, but his fear had turned to pleasure. Billy Sky had taught him most of what he knew about stalking, silence, and observation. If Billy Sky wanted to get drunk within a hundred yards of the house and not be bothered by the Brigadier's demands, which he occasionally did, neither the Brigadier nor Meade could find him. He was a natural. He loved the General fiercely, for God knew what reason. The man had tormented and ordered Billy around since the Indian had been in the old man's command in the Pacific. After Meade's mother had died, Billy had been cook, nurse, and teacher to the listless young man. He'd helped him build model ships late on winter evenings while his father built furniture in the garage. But Meade had no illusions. If he'd threatened the Brigadier at all during that conversation in the garage, Billy Sky would have lit him up without thinking.

Like most Indians he wasted no time chatting. "I'll see to the dogs, sir. 'Night, Junior."

"Good night, Billy." He followed his father up the severely straight path to the house, knowing Billy was not going to be far away.

Meade sat in the den of the old place, its knotty-pine paneling, dark with age, still glowed with care and polish. In the corner the Brigadier's pine desk was arranged with military precision; a 105 howitzer shell casing for an ashtray, a Chinese officer's dagger for a letter opener. The flags of battalions he'd commanded furled on pikes behind the desk. Meade sat by the fire roaring in the big hearth, in an armchair sporting a print of flushed pheasants. His father poured two large tumblers half full of Wild Turkey. He walked over and handed one to Meade. He took a perch on the edge of his desk, his long legs stretched out before him. Meade took a large swallow. He shuddered at the power of the whiskey, but it warmed him inside. He hadn't realized how cold he'd felt.

"How's business?"

"Not bad," the Brigadier replied, sipping. "Right now I've only got three dogs in for training. Almost all of the rest are gone. It's bird season everywhere, and training is over for the year. We've got three litters of pointers, though—several of them are first class. The best bitches now go for eight hundred dollars—without training. I can't complain."

The business boomed even when Meade was in military school before his father's "retirement" from the service. He flew in English pointers from around the country, to be bred, and he had started the kennel by keeping the picks of litters. He'd known the right people at the AKC and soon got his own breeders' licence, raising the nervous, hard-hunting dogs with scrupulous care, destroying puppies, and even whole litters on occasion, when the breeding had taken a bad turn. And then he'd advertised in the hunting magazines and had built a busy, mail-order empire of English pointers.

Summers, when upward of three-dozen dogs were shipped out to Montana for training—the other half of the business—it was Meade's job to do airport runs, meeting the Northwest flights, shipping out English pointer pups in their steel mesh cages, and picking up half-crazed hunting dogs of many breeds coming in for training at upland bird hunting. It was costly, too. But the Brigadier rarely failed. If he found a dog that was truly gun-shy, or could not be trained to hold a point, or who repeatedly bayed after deer and raccoons when it was supposed to keep its mind on quail and grouse and woodcock, the Brigadier would ship the dog back to the owner with merely a bill for board and feed, suggesting that the owner have the dog neutered or spayed to preserve the breed from a basically chickenshit attitude. It was a hard business, right up the Brigadier's alley.

"Why did you come home, J. R.?"

"To get Hannah and then get out. I guess I stopped to say good-bye to you."

"I hope you didn't come around with some half-baked notion that I'd forgive you or something. I'm not very good at this sort of thing." The Brigadier ran his large hand over his short hair. "Maybe that's been the problem sometimes between us. But you've gone and done something for which there's no turning back. I can't condone it."

"You've spent a lot of your life judging other people, General. That's the real problem. Maybe that was the problem with my mother."

The Brigadier rose and sat behind his desk. It was as if he knew what was coming and was taking cover. "We've had this talk once before," he said evenly. "Your mother was an alcoholic. I've seen it too often in the army. It's an illness. We did everything we could, but the sickness won out. I don't know why you've blamed me all these years, J. R. It's childish."

"What caused her to become an alcoholic, then?"

"You're sitting there with a drink now. If anyone had reason to drown his troubles in drink, I'd think it would be you. But you won't. Neither will I. Some people just can't resist the stuff. It's as simple as that. Grow up, J. R. You've been through a war, for Christ's sake. Distinguished yourself, too. You know as well as I do that most things have no reason. Someone dies and someone doesn't. Who the hell's to blame? You said that I spent my life judging people, maybe that's true. But you've spent a decade judging me, and what's it done for either of us?" The Brigadier took a long pull on the bourbon and toyed with the Chinese knife.

"You weren't here. That's why she drank. You were a colonel then. You spent most of the year at Fort Reilly in Kansas, trying to make general staff, busting your ass for a star. We were here in those winters. God, it was awful. She'd drink and watch the snow blow across the yard. Sometimes I'd come home from school on the bus and find her sound asleep in the living room. She had accidents all the time, burning herself on the stove, cutting her fingers with cooking knives. It was a torture. And in the end the goddamn general staff gave you a star, General. But they wouldn't give you two, to make you a major general. And you did the honorable thing. Resigned. It was all for nothing."

The Brigadier's head was bowed for a moment. Meade wondered if he'd wounded him. He wondered if that's why he'd come here in the first place. He didn't think so. But he needn't have worried. The Brigadier was a tough piece of work. "Your mother and I made a peace with that long ago, J. R. I wanted to be a general. The army was my life. As you know, general staff is more than just rising from colonel. They want you to be the 'right' kind of man." The Brigadier snorted and took a long pull on his drink. "And part of that is having a so-called happy home life. Your mother hated the army life and just didn't want to hang around the base and be the Brigadier's 'lady.' So she stayed out here with you."

"But it was all a waste, General."

"I suppose so, but you can only learn from your losses, not hang over them being an armchair strategist of your own life."

"They passed you over twice for the second star."

"The army had its reasons."

"The army is always right, I suppose? Are you going to pull that crap after Nam?" Meade flushed with the argument, trying to win something he was not sure of.

"I wasn't the right material for staff. They were right about that. Perhaps I should have resigned earlier, but what the hell was the use?" The Brigadier stared reflectively into his drink for a moment and then smiled at Meade, enjoying, perhaps, his discomfort. "But that's old history, boy. What about you? Look at you."

The Brigadier stared at the shabby, lumpy, scratch-bearded figure in the wire-frame glasses dressed for winter fly fishing. He walked over to the wall of the den, on which were hung two dozen photographs of different sizes, black-and-white prints, framed in thin black wood. He surveyed the wall. The life history of J. R. Meade. There was a pose of Meade dressed in a Missoula junior high football uniform, looking gawky, vacant, and adolescent. Another was Meade with his mother, a thin, spectral woman in a black Chanel suit and pearls and white gloves and hat, taken on the steps of Oake Hall at Virginia Military Academy. Meade, diploma in hand, crisp in his summer dress uniform, towered over her, looking properly martial for an eighteen-year-old. And finally there was the eight by ten, now famous around the country, of Meade in his green beret, looking smooth-skinned, ready, and tough. The Brigadier shook his head.

"Why the hell did you do it, boy?"

"Because I've been trained to." Meade didn't know *why* he'd done it, beyond wanting to get his sloop and sail out on the Pacific forever, unhassled, no orders, avoiding pursuit.

"Don't give me sociology, Sergeant. You did it because you wanted to make a goddamn stink. I saw your service record, the FBI inspector had that much respect for my former rank. Good God, if I'd been your commanding officer you'd have been out of the army long before you shipped overseas. You've got some need to show everybody how damn good you are at tactics. Tactics don't win wars. Only battles. Strategy wins wars." The Brigadier paced the room, his hands clasped behind his back as if giving a lecture to a group of junior officers, Meade thought.

"I did it because it was the right thing to do. I want out of this shit, General, out of a bureaucracy that stops good men, that makes women become alcoholics, that sends little kids ten thousand miles to fight people that have no grievance, because I . . ."

"Enough. Just enough." The Brigadier sat down in the chair opposite the fireplace, and looked across the few feet that was an immeasurable gulf between them. His face showed emotions and thoughts that Meade had not known existed in the man. And his words were halting, as if he'd entered new territory without a map. "J. R., I think maybe we're not so different. We're both better at action than at thinking things through. You were that way as a kid. A lousy quarterback. You couldn't call plays worth a goddamn, but you could execute them. In the long run that's why I'm out here running dogs through training instead of commanding a division of men, and that's why you're going to be running the rest of your life. I can't come to terms with what you've done, boy, but I'm glad you're good at it."

Meade said nothing; he finished his drink. Maybe it had all been said. The tension was gone. Two men having a drink before a fireplace in a Montana farmhouse. That's what it came to. Meade toyed with an old leather dog lead he'd found by the chair, tying knots in it and untying them. It was his form of doodling.

"Stay the night, J. R. Get a bath and a shave, and new clothes if you want them. Your old room is still upstairs."

"I don't think I'd better, General, the FBI and a man named Gruen are out there."

"Gruen? Oh, yes, that aviation investigator, I've seen him on the news."

"He was my top in Vietnam."

"My God. Special Forces?"

"He taught me how to do it. He's the best they've got and I'll bet the son of a bitch is around. He won't fall for the FBI idea of guarding borders."

"I don't want to know your plans, J. R. But Billy Sky is out there. Special Forces doesn't get by him and that riot gun." Meade was touched. His father was offering him protection.

There was an ancient test of friendship. When they were kids, just learning to touch each other, to grind their lips together dryly and hold hands, Hannah had asked him one day in that innocence of teen-age ideas of loyalty, "If I'd murdered somebody and the police were after me, would you hide me?" Meade had answered sure. And he meant it. Hannah said, "Me too." He wondered if she still would. And he'd never thought his father would have done it. Although the house wasn't safe, anyone could be watching, even the FBI for all their claims of forgetting Missoula. It was a risk Meade gladly took. It was the price of sailing away with a clearer conscience.

His room on the second floor of the house was much as it had been when he was a boy. Wood and plastic model ships, many of them askew and bubbly with glue, sat on the bookshelves, a testimony to his fascination with the sea, although his youthful impatience was noticeable in their lack of craftsmanship. His bed was too short for him now. He lay in it, after a hot bath and wearing a pair of his father's fresh pajamas. He smiled; the pajamas were starched. The army takes hold of a man like the Brigadier, and doesn't let go in some ways. Tomorrow morning, before first light, he'd be up and back in his fishing outfit, out of the house. He wanted no good-bye with the old man. At least not yet. There was Hannah to take care of. Or she'd take care of him. Meade arranged the survival knife, strapping the scabbard to the leg of the bed, near his hand but out of sight of the door. He'd taken the precaution of picking up one of the old man's .45s from the den gun case. It was loaded and Meade had quietly jacked a shell into the chamber. It lay cocked on the wall side of the bed. As he drifted into a light sleep, he grinned in the dark room. Forgiveness was all well and good, and Billy Sky was out there somewhere in the shadows, a slug of Tokay in his throat and that huge elephant gun ready to blow the moon in half if necessary, but it was best to be cautious. The old man was right—they were good at details.

5
HANNAH

As he reached the highway and turned toward the Lolo Pass Road the following morning Gruen regretted the two years he'd wasted behind a desk. He'd have to say one thing for that goddamn Meade; he'd gotten Gruen's blood moving, his brain working, and his pecker up.

When Gruen wheeled into Don Tripp's Truck Palace he was humming and ready for the immense breakfast the place was famous for. Later he headed for Upland Farms to meet the Brigadier, the eggs and ham and hash-browns weighing him down; singing "Hello, Walls," a simple-minded country-and-western song about loneliness, beating time on the wheel.

At the end of the long, straight gravel road that led off the county highway back to the Brigadier's place, Gruen understood what they meant by "Big Sky" country. Towering thunderheads boiled up in the clear blue bell of the sky between the mountains for thousands of feet, casting long, swiftly moving shadows which rushed across the meadows and fields, sweeping over a man like a final judgment and disappearing just as swiftly, leaving him in dazzling sunshine listening to the song birds calling from the grain fields.

As he had at Hannah's, Gruen sat in the van in the agonizingly neat farmyard and beeped the horn. Two huskies rested on their tailbones, staring at him. He tooted again before a pot-bellied Indian walked around the corner of a shed carrying a sawed-off riot gun. Montana had more firearms than good sense, Gruen thought. Everyone in the state seemed to be armed to the teeth. That old buck could blow a hole right through his door with that piece. Gruen regretted not carrying a gun himself, but he felt foolish being armed in a place where there were no Koreans or Vietnamese. But he'd better get on the stick or he'd get dead.

"I've come to see Brigadier Meade," Gruen said through the slit he'd opened in the van window, holding his ID card against the glass. The Indian didn't even glance at the card. "Wait here," he said, and disappeared behind a long, low building. In a moment the Brigadier appeared, dressed in a goose-down vest against the chill and wearing thin, deerskin gloves.

"Come on out. Billy and the dogs won't bother you. You're from the FAA, Mr. Gruen?"

He was stunned. "I didn't think your man with the shotgun even looked at my ID." Gruen felt a cautious elation. If the Brigadier knew who he was, maybe Meade had told him. And recently. But the Brigadier shattered his joy. "You're quite famous. Billy Sky can read checks and count money. But ID never much impressed him. We've all seen your face on television and in the papers. You're the headhunter who's after my son."

"Not exactly. I don't bring 'em in tied to the saddle, General."

"You were a sergeant in Special Forces, so the papers said."

Gruen slipped easily, like an old pack horse, into the bureaucratic harness of the service. This was a general. "Yes, sir, I was. But it's pure coincidence that we've come to this, uh, this state of affairs." The old man was not going to give away anything. Gruen could tell that he hadn't been the kind of officer who left the running of a unit to his noncoms. He was a tough old turkey, and a smart one. The FBI report had shown him to be reasonably cooperative, but the investigating agent had noted that there was a coolness toward authority in the Brigadier, a reserve. After all, Meade was his son, no matter what the Brigadier said about duty and patriotism. But Gruen had to find out for himself.

"If you want to talk, you'll have to join me. It's time to feed the dogs." The Brigadier turned and walked quickly into the long, Butler building. They emerged on the other side of the structure, the Brigadier wheeling a cart bearing several different mixes of fifty-pound bags of dog meal and a large steel water tank. They walked along before the row of fenced-in dog runs, the big clouds rushing over their heads. There were a dozen dogs; big, healthy hunting breeds: an Irish setter, a pair of weimaraners, a few pointers of various breeds. They began barking and leaping when they spotted the Brigadier with the food cart. On the door of each run was a plastic envelope containing a five by seven card with information about the dog inside, including diet, owner, training, age, and other statistics. The Brigadier consulted the first one, an English pointer whose whiplike tail thrashed wildly as the animal jumped several feet in the air in pure nervous joy. The Brigadier took the stainless-steel feed dish from the pen through a small sliding door in the bottom of the larger chain-link gate and began to fill it with a mixture of feeds from his cart.

"I told the FBI all I know, Sergeant. I can't think of anything you'd want that isn't in their report."

Gruen thought there was no reason to dick around with this hard old case. "I'm an inspector for the Federal Aviation Agency, I'm not an army sergeant any longer, General. And there's one question the FBI hasn't asked you in a while. Have you seen your son recently?"

"No," the Brigadier barked. But his remark was for the dog whom he was shooing back from the small trap door where it had been trying to squirm through, its tail walloping the concrete. "I haven't seen him since he left for Alaska eight months ago, ah, Inspector."

They walked on to the next pen. "The two of you must have an uneasy relationship. I mean, your son turned down Officer Candidate School, went into the army as a recruit, after VMI and all. And then the skyjacking."

The Brigadier stopped filling a dog bowl and looked evenly at Gruen, controlling his anger.

"Inspector, children, and if you have any you know what I mean, often do what's unexpected and unacceptable to their parents. It's partly to twist the knife and it's partly stubbornness. This family has been a stubborn one, and J. R. merely carried it into another generation. That doesn't necessarily make an 'uneasy relationship' as you call it, and it won't make me inform on my son either."

"You told the FBI that you'd inform them if your son contacted you. Have you changed your mind?"

"When did you resign from the army, Gruen?"

"Four years ago, why?"

"It was ten years ago when I resigned a commission. Do you know why?"

"Yes, I've seen the file."

"I don't feel I owe the government much. They used me for thirty years and then failed to reward me with a second star, when I saw lesser men getting them. Men with connections, friends, politicians of the Pentagon. So don't bother to appeal to my patriotism."

Gruen felt a flicker of sympathy with the Brigadier. "I can see what you mean, General. They put me out to pasture too, recruitment division. I was just a chest full of medals giving talks in high schools. But that doesn't change what your son did. It's a felony, sir, and he's going to get caught. If I take him, he's got a fair chance of going to prison. There's a number of amateurs and volunteers looking for him, and they're not going to be so gentle. If you know where he is, you'd be doing him a favor. Saving his life maybe. That money's going to bring the hounds from everywhere."

"Possibly, but you underestimate J. R., Inspector. You people trained him pretty well. I don't think you'll get him."

"And you're going to help him, I take it?"

"I want you to see something, Gruen." The Brigadier led the way to a pen on the end of the line where a thin-boned Irish setter banged her tail against the chain-link fence. She sunk low to the ground as the Brigadier approached. He walked up to the fence and stared at the dog. The Brigadier slowly raised his hands and clapped them loudly and sharply. The dog scrabbled on the concrete, leaving a dribble of urine as she threw herself against the back of the run twenty-five feet away from them, quivering and shaking, whimpering softly. The Brigadier turned to Gruen, sadness in his eyes.

"That animal cost a thousand dollars. She's from the best setter kennels in America, impeccable breeding, a list of studs and dams that have more AKC championships than you can count. An animal bred to hunt and love it, to live for nothing else except the hunt.

"And we knew she was a nervous dog when she ar-

rived here. We gave her extra time to calm down. We
trained her gently and slowly. She responded well. She
could set a covey of quail prettier than anything you've
ever seen. It made you proud that God had put dogs on
earth when she worked. She casted out from you at
exactly the right distance and angles. She was perfection
itself. And we slowly worked her with the gun. Letting
her see it and smell it and know perfectly well it was part
of the hunt. Billy Sky would fire a little .410 one hundred
yards from her and reward her, and over the course of a
week, he'd worked the gun in on her. She seemed fine.
Finally we hunted her with the gun, with some quail
we'd set. That's part of the training. And when Billy
took a bird right over her, she broke. She just lay down
and wouldn't get up. A gun-shy animal.

"Who knows what causes such a thing? Something
just went in her brain or her blood, some old line of
genes that couldn't take the noise of a shotgun." The
Brigadier opened the big door of the pen and gently,
his hand extended, called the dog over. She came hes-
itantly toward him and he squatted and petted her,
holding her. He turned to Gruen, the animal's frightened
eyes rolling toward the Inspector. "And what am I to do
with her? I'll send a letter to her owner explaining the
situation. Advising that he have her spayed immediately.
She's no good for the breed. But no one wants to shoot
her, or put her away. She's got some usefulness. I've seen
it happen in the army, too. A man on paper will look
like General Sherman himself and turn out to be a
coward or a fuck-up or idiot. And you don't throw them
in the stockade. You make the best of it. They have
their uses."

"You're saying your son's just a misfit and to let him
go, aren't you?"

"I just told you the story about dogs, Mr. Gruen. Make

of it what you will." The Brigadier turned and began filling the setter's bowl with food.

Gruen asked to use the telephone, and Billy Sky, who materialized from a doorway when the Brigadier spoke his name, led Gruen into the den of the big comfortable farmhouse. Gruen called the Great Falls FBI office for developments. There were none. Another dozen reports of Meade being seen in all places from New Orleans to Montreal were checking out false. That was all. Of course that was all, Gruen thought as he hung up the phone. He was more convinced than ever that Meade was headed to Missoula. Probably there right now.

On his way out of the room, accompanied by Billy Sky, who'd politely left the .10-gauge behind somewhere, Gruen stopped to admire a big oil painting over the mantel that depicted a pair of English pointers working a meadow in late fall with a profusion of brown grass and changing leaves in the background and a hunter with raised gun pointing at a streaking quail. Gruen glanced at the hearth and his heart froze.

Lying by an easy chair was a nearly new leather dog lead. Not an unusual item for a kennel. But precisely in the middle of the leash was a perfectly tied sheepshank. A knot Gruen knew, used in the army to shorten loose lines, with distinctive double loops coming from it. There was no need to tie one on a dog lead. Only someone who kept his hands busy tying knots would have tied a sheepshank with something near at hand. The Brigadier wasn't the type. Very recently, J. R. Meade had sat in that chair. Gruen had been right. He showed nothing to Billy Sky as he walked out of the door.

Backing the van around to drive away, the Indian and the two huskies watched him like three old sentries, bored but alert. Gruen's mind was racing. He wasn't going to let the FBI in on this. He'd rub their noses in it.

He just had to work out how to get Meade. Hannah was the key now; the son of a bitch had already seen his father. He turned onto the black top and headed for his motel. The first thing to do was to get his gun.

"Jesus!" Mason Remson jumped up from the barstool as if shot. Two stools away from him in Eddie's Club in downtown Missoula a drunk had passed out, his forehead hitting the bar with a riflelike crack. Remson had just been mulling over how he'd take Meade, a little fantasy to accompany the first tequila of the day, and he'd had a vision of J. R. Meade, in Special Forces uniform, crossing his rifle sights, when the drunk's head smashed the bar, filling him with the same kind of terror that incoming rounds from the faceless jungle in Nam created in him.

Remson had gone into a crouch, his hands raised in the clawlike motions of self-defense, ready to tear anyone to pieces. His eyes were opaque, a low smile cracking his blotched face. The bartender walked down the bar wiping his hands on a towel. He raised the drunk's head with a mother's tenderness and opened an eyelid, staring into the blank gaze professionally. The comatose man had wispy gray hair, a face the color of beefsteak, and wore dirty clothes. A fine line of foamy spittle ran from the corner of his mouth. He was one of those men in whose face you could tell how they looked as a child when they slept, an innocence of bones and flesh in their faces shedding the years of adulthood.

The bartender took a stack of beer-moist bills and a pile of change from beneath the man's head and gently lowered him back down on the bar. He turned to a small, antique safe behind the bar, opened the door, and selected a white envelope from a tall stack. He counted the old man's money carefully, put it in the envelope, and returned it to the safe.

"You're a little jumpy, there, pard." He looked with amusement at Remson.

"Let's have another shot." Remson had heard about Eddie's Club from a few of the old timers at his flophouse hotel, a place where a working man or a retired fella from the Great Northern or, for Christ's sake, even an Indian, didn't get cheated, they'd told him. Old cowboys and sheepmen and railroad fellas came to town to get roar-ass drunk and you could hand over your stake to the bartender and he'd keep it for you in the safe, letting you drink it up and even extending a little credit on the shy side if he knew you well enough. They wouldn't let you gamble on the cuff at the endless poker games at the huge, round tables in the back room, however. They wouldn't even let drunks in the game.

The bartender returned with a shot of tequila, and Remson gulped it down in one swallow. The bartender didn't raise an eyebrow. The drunk began to snore.

"You gonna leave him there all day?"

"I've known this boy for thirty years, pard. In about ten minutes he'll wake up, have a cup of coffee with schnapps, and drink us all under the table."

Remson was disgusted. He was a drinker, maybe an evil drunk the way the goddamn army told it, but he didn't pass out at the bar. And he kept himself in pretty good shape, too. But it was time to work, now. If he scored, and he was sure he would, there'd be no more flophouses, no more cheap saloons full of goodwill. He'd be set up in a good apartment in L.A. with the best Scotch and the prettiest women and spend the day at the track. He regarded the bartender. A bland-looking man, but the huge biceps on him made Remson go slowly.

"Any of these old boys ever carry guns? You check 'em in like the Wild West?"

The bartender cocked his head. "Oh, now and then an Indian might try to pull a piece and fuck things up, but it's against the law to carry guns in town."

"You mean you don't need a permit?" Remson was stunned.

"Hell, no, man, this ain't Massachusetts. The Bill of Rights says you can bear arms, and by God, most of us bear 'em!"

"You mean I can walk into a store and buy a rifle or a shotgun and I don't need a permit?"

"No, but you gotta show some ID. They don't like to sell 'em to kids."

"Pistols, I guess, are restricted."

"Why?" The bartender was genuinely perplexed. "Restricted to what?" Remson smiled and ordered another shot. This Montana was all right. He'd check out the local hardware on his way out of town. On the way to see Mrs. J. R. Meade. That son of a bitch Meade was nearby, Remson could smell it, could taste him, and that money. It was a matter of being at the right place at the right time, and Remson knew how to do that. A good many unlucky VC suspects in the hamlets had discovered that. You didn't fuck around with Corporal Mason Remson.

He took the piece of yellow paper he'd ripped from the phonebook. "River Trips, Inc." It had a little map that showed how to get right to Mrs. Meade. Remson thought she might talk to him. Hell, he smiled to himself, she'll sing the fucking national anthem when I get through with her.

As Remson walked to the door, the bartender picked up his empty glass. He found a penny for a tip. The bartender said to the snoring drunk, "That's one bad little prick there, my friend. A motherless child. He won't drink in here again."

"Hello. Is this Hannah Meade?"

"Yes?" She was out of breath, running to the house from the raft barn, where she'd been painting paddles. She grimaced. Paint had gotten on the handset of the phone. Something else to clean up out here. It was almost coffee-break time anyway. She poured a cup, careful not to get paint on the pot handle as she cradled the phone to her ear with her shoulder.

"Well, Hannah, it's good to hear your voice after all these years," said the man's voice. It sounded like he had a cold.

"Who is this?"

"It's Tommy Trader from high school, remember? I'm calling about the class reunion. I hope you'll come." Hannah almost laughed out loud. Tommy Trader was the private name she and Meade had given to an old man who lived near the Brigadier's place, long dead now, who traded one useless object for another with amused local farmers. He'd trade an old bathtub for a worn-out tractor tire, or a crank telephone for a bushel of apples. The local folks kept him in food; he was harmless and carried a lot of broken information from farm to farm. He lived in a rundown shack and after he died, Hannah and Meade as young teens would often play there, rummaging through the piles of junk and petting in the evenings.

"Oh, dear Hannah, you really slipped up." Meade in a disguised voice—she could picture him somewhere, holding his nose with his fingers—said, "It's tonight, ten o'clock. Can you come? It would sure be good to see you again." So he wanted to meet her at the Trader's place tonight. She started to go over the list of reasons that she should tell him to go to hell. Whatever Meade had in mind it was going to be complicated emotionally, unsettling physically, and probably dangerous and illegal to boot. "I'll be there," she said.

"Ohh, that's wonderful, Hannah. So many of your old friends from high school will just be dying to know what you've been up to all these years." She hung up the phone. Maybe that big bastard Gruen had been right. Maybe Meade wasn't worth the trouble. Maybe he would get caught and spend his life in prison. She could hear the old clock on the mantel, tolling out the minutes from the living room in the silent house. The refrigerator clicked on.

But Meade seemed better right now than an empty house all winter, and the occasional meeting with a stranger like Gruen you could grow to like. She didn't want to become a horny old maid of the River, raping men who floated by, and living alone, mumbling to herself, mending rafts and paddles. And who could resist the arrogant son of a bitch, wanted all over the world, holding his nose to confuse the wire tap if there was one, calling himself Tommy Trader? It had probably worked, too.

That was always the surprising thing about Meade. He didn't make any mistakes. Except about her. But maybe coming here when so many people were after him was trying to right that wrong. Whatever happened she'd better tell the Brigadier. The phone might not, indeed, be safe, and as she gathered up her bag and car keys, she sensed an excitement that she hadn't felt in a long time. Too long a time.

Meade lay back on the bed in room 109 of the Big Sky Motel, on the Missoula Strip, after hanging up the telephone. He was now Albert F. C. Clarke, of FlinFlon, Manitoba, sales manager of western Canada for Wayne Feeds. He had a razored haircut, administered by an Italian barber in Last Dance; he had false ID, carefully forged on a trip to Alberta two years ago; and he was dressed for the part. He wore a polyester gray suit, with a vest, cut in the "gentleman's Western" style, with lots of saddle stitching. The breast pocket of the coat was stuffed with Roi-Tan cigars. Beside the bed stood two-hundred-dollar Justin antelope-skin cowboy boots. Three pieces of plastic luggage stood in the corner. Meade looked at his reflection in the mirror over the dresser opposite the bed and waved to himself. He tried on the large, black-framed sunglasses and stuck one of the cigars, still in its cellophane wrapper, into his mouth. "Goddamn, but I can move that feed, eh?" He tried out his flat Canadian accent with that curious "eh" on the end of the sentence. He thought it was passable, at least in Missoula. He'd moved in that morning, all jolly and high-pressured and back slapping, demanding the best double room that the motel had, with a wink to the desk man, and asked advice on the best steakhouse and best bars and where the action was. He was not surprised to learn that the desk man, a fortyish mousey man, had directed him to all the wrong places.

He had sweated out the call to Hannah, and was elated that she would meet him. According to the paper he'd bought that morning, Inspector William Gruen was still in Missoula, "investigating leads," which was the way the reporter said he didn't know what the hell Gruen was up to. Meade did, though. Gruen was using that well-trained army nose to sniff him out. It was an old exercise from Vietnam, locating the VC in a village, hootch by hootch, relative by relative, often a tangled and torturous path of relationships, observations, and deductions. Meade had been good at it. Gruen was just as good. Often it was the detail escaping someone else's attention that would do it: a shell casing from an AK-47 Russian-made rifle in the corner of a hootch; quickly smelling a man's hands in a rice paddy for the telltale odor of cordite. It was a shitty job, but it was necessary, the army said. As he thought, Meade played with the curtain cord at the side of the bed, tying a bowline around his finger with his left hand, looping a sheepshank, throwing it into a square knot and half hitches. He'd have to watch himself carefully with Gruen around.

Outside the motel, supersalesman Meade, puffing on a cigar, got into the big, black Pontiac he'd rented at the airport with his new driver's license and Master Charge card. After all, the district manager of Wayne Feeds had to travel in style, and he didn't lie around motels all day, either. Time to get to work. Meade heaved the heavy salesman's sample case onto the seat and climbed in. Time to make a deposit. Time was money, so they said in the office. Time was a river that slipped away, they said that too. Meade was glad that he didn't work in an office, where people said shit like that.

Gruen sat in the van, honking the horn. The husky looked professionally bored. Gruen could see that Hannah's car was missing from the garage. He had the wild idea that she'd already left with Meade, flown. In the glove box, his Smith and Wesson .38 lay like a tumor. He knew ways to undo that dog without using the gun, but he didn't want to snap its neck and have Hannah come back from a grocery run to find him ransacking the house and her dog dead. Besides Meade wouldn't hang around such an obvious spot during the day. He thought carefully. It was three miles to the Brigadier's spread.

It wouldn't do to drive there again, with the hostility and that Indian with the shotgun. When he'd been there earlier, he'd spotted a rise behind the house. He'd have to drive the road in back of the spread and come through there if he could, without running into one of those damn dogs. He backed out and headed for the Brigadier's.

Mason Remson came out of the Missoula Mercantile store with three packages. One contained a Remington .303 with a Weaver 5X telescopic sight, and the other contained a Smith and Wesson .38 police special with a five-inch barrel, and the third contained a box of shells for each gun. Just as the bartender had said, no one asked him a thing. He'd picked out the firearms, waited while the scope was mounted on the high-powered rifle, and walked out with his packages as if he were going to a birthday party. In a way it was, Remson smiled. He was giving himself a present of $750,000.

Remson walked quickly toward his car a block away on the long, low main street of Missoula, where the pawn shops melted into tacky bars and fly-specked restaurants. Remson was suddenly brought up short. Sauntering toward him down the street was a willowy hippie, long blond hair below his shoulders and a wisp of beard growing from the spot between his chin and his lower lip. His corduroy pants were several sizes too large and were held up with an old necktie. In deference to the November chill, the boy, who looked to be in his early twenties, wore thick white socks with his sandals. But what stopped Remson was the picture on the T-shirt across the kid's scrawny chest, visible under his open pea coat. It was a silk-screened picture of J. R. Meade, wearing his green beret, the picture that the newspapers and the FBI had made famous.

Remson was dumbfounded. He'd been in Vietnam through the turmoil of the late sixties, and in Mexico during the wild fashion swings of the seventies. One thing that awed him were T-shirts, like the one he'd seen a girl wearing that morning, a young big-chested thing with the legend "Texas Grapefruits," with arrows pointing to her unbound breasts.

Remson reached out a hand like a traffic cop and stopped the young man. "Say, where'd you get that shirt, man?"

"Oh, uh." The boy looked down at his chest as if surprised to find that it existed. He wiped a few long strands of hair back over his ear. "I *think*, at the Full Moon Head Shop." Above the picture of Meade on the shirt were the words: "He's The One!"

"You like this guy, Meade, huh?" Remson was appalled at the boy and the shirt. There was a menace in his tone that the boy picked up on right away.

"Well, ya; he's pretty nifty. Ripped off the establishment and they're never going to catch him. He's too smart and too good. He's like a kind of political Patty Hearst, you know?"

"No. I don't know. What the hell are you talking about? He's a goddamn thief, a criminal, and somebody's gonna nail him, boy." Remson gripped his packages tightly, advancing on the kid. The boy began to backpedal quickly. He turned and broke into a soft trot, his hair swinging as he looked back over his shoulder at Remson.

Fuckin' hippies, know-it-all bastards, wouldn't fight the war and when I did my job they threw me out of the service because of these bleeding hearts at home. And now the little prick thinks Mr. Wise-ass is a great guy. Remson slammed into his car, checked the map against the torn-out ad from the Yellow Pages, and headed out of town.

When Hannah came out of the house at nine-thirty in the darkness, the husky was sitting in the driveway, looking in the direction of the river, whimpering. "What's the matter, Nelson? You never whine." The dog leaned against her leg and accepted her petting, without relaxing his vigilance. "Maybe you know your master's near, huh? Maybe you'll see him tonight." When she drove off a moment later, the dog was still staring toward the roaring Clark Fork, its white foam visible leaping over the boulders fifty yards away, as the taillights of Hannah's car disappeared down the driveway.

Across the river on the rise of the bank Mason Remson had knelt in the darkness, hurting his knee on a pile of high-powered bullet jackets. Some fool out target practicing, no doubt. He shifted and waited, watching the windows of the house as it grew dark, watched the lights come on, watched the woman move through the rooms, saw her sit alone in the kitchen, eating her supper while reading a book, saw her come out into the yard, a good-looking broad if you liked them big and blond and stacked like an F-104. She petted her dog and headed for her car. Remson took off in a crouching sprint for his own rented car. He'd have to double back almost a quarter mile to get across the river to her side again, over a private farm bridge.

When he turned onto the highway, a few moments later, he could make out the taillights of a car just disappearing over a dark rise to the east. He smiled in the dark interior of the car and began humming "Che sarà, sarà" while he fumbled for the half pint of tequila that should be somewhere beside him on the seat. His fingers fumbled over the .38, cold to the touch. It was almost as good as the liquor.

Hannah pulled off the dirt road that led by Tommy Trader's old place into the twin, weed-filled ruts that led back to the shack. Tommy had died several years ago, shortly after she graduated from high school. He had been found by a group of boys on their way fishing in a little creek behind the place, his body tipped into an old, claw-foot bathtub full of rainwater in his yard. A small anvil was wrapped around his neck with a length of greasy rope. Tommy had committed an ugly, second-hand suicide. What sadness could have lurked in that slightly askew but jolly man? Maybe it was living in this place.

Hannah parked in the shack's overgrown front yard, her headlights illuminating the wild wreckage. It was impossible to guess what damage had been done by marauding boys and what was due to the old man's negligence. The shack was made of logs, tarpaper, cardboard, bark, mud, and newspapers. There was a shallow porch that ran along the front of the one-room building, where the dirty burlap window coverings blew in the November wind.

The whole front of the shack and the yard as far as her headlights shone was a mad jumble of things broken, dirty, rusted, and twisted: washing machines; antlers; parts of motors and engines; a huge cable drum; tangles of wire and rope; two totem poles, their animal heads evil in the half light; nail kegs; beer bottles in shreds of paper bags; rags; clothing; an airplane wing; and a very old, rusted fire truck, the gilt lettering on the door too faded to read, hose rotted away, tire gone, stripped of lights and siren, only the windshield incredibly intact. It had been there since Hannah was a child, and probably before. She grinned dumbly at it. It had been on the ripped and cracked leather of its front seat, where the springs and the horsehair stuffing stuck through in itchy, painful tufts, that she had first kissed, petted, and made love, with a silent, serious boy who wanted to sail around the world when he grew up.

There was no sign of a car. She switched off the lights and waited, thinking that the trouble with J. R. Meade was that he hadn't grown up, inside at least. She felt sentimental, sitting in Tommy Trader's yard, her thoughts as confused and jumbled as the old man's collection of useless objects. But then, she thought, everybody grew up and that was boring. Maybe it was better to have a serious child around who loved her in his drifting, absent way, full of plans and strange impulses, back from the war he hated.

"Hey, lady, got ten dollars for a cup of coffee?" She jumped and hit her head on the car roof. The dark figure by her window looked in, smiling.

"Jesus Christ! Meade? Why the hell do you always do that? What are you dressed like that for?" Her questions rushed out in a torrent of irritation, pent up for the past eight months, locked away in daily routine without him.

Meade in his western-style suit said, "The name's Albert F. C. Clarke from FlinFlon, little gal." He threw the cigar stub away into the tangle of objects behind him.

"How are you, Hannah?" He spoke with a gentleness

that at first softened her, and then fanned her sense of outrage. "Oh, I'm just fine, I love it when you're rough."

"I can't stand out here all night while you have a snit," Meade said quietly. "And I can't be too careful right now. Come on over in the fire truck." Meade opened her door and took her hand. It was cold. She was trembling slightly. He didn't know if it was from the chill in the night air, or from emotions. "Come on."

She walked with him, like they'd done as kids, she thought, with Meade leading her to the rusted, cannibalized hulk of the fire truck, but so much was different now than then. Climbing into the cab of the wreck, the familiar odors were quickly apparent: rust, mildew, leather. It was cold, and she pulled her goose-down coat more tightly around herself. Meade swung up into the driver's seat from the opposite side and sat staring out through the windshield.

"There's all sort of things I want to say, Hannah," he said evenly, but all the explanations that he'd rehearsed over the weeks since he jumped from the 727 had flown from him. "Look, it seems I've come into some money, and I'm going sailing. I want you to come with me. It wouldn't be much fun without you."

She controlled the torrent of ideas and questions that filled her mind. "Going to sail around the world, Meade, like you planned?"

"That's the idea, love. I really need somebody to haul up sails and take the wheel."

"That's what you need, huh?"

"Come on," he said impatiently, reaching out across the dark seat and taking her hand, "you know it's more than that."

"Meade, it's out of a fairy tale. People don't go play Robin Hood, or whatever you thought you were doing, and then go sail around the world. It just doesn't fit in reality."

"I saw enough reality in Vietnam, Hannah, and it's a question for some philosophy professor on a government grant. Besides I'm counting on the fact that the FBI and that goddamned Gruen will think the same thing. They want logic, so I've got to give them something else. Something they can't expect."

"Meade, you've been a drifter since I've known you. A natural mover. I don't think I'm the type to stick it out, sailing around the world, assuming that we even got that far. You can't believe the number of people who want to catch you. I'm a homebody, J. R. I like my cabin on the river. I even enjoy the business, too. What I want is for you to stick around for more than two weeks at a time and settle down."

"Well, I can't do that now. And you'd be home on the boat. We'd both be happy. I'd be there all the time. It's just that home would move across the water."

She turned in the seat and took his strong face in her hands. "Oh, Meade, I want to, more than anything. But a life on the run . . . Oh, damn." Meade bent to kiss her and she tilted her head up to him.

The windshield of the fire truck exploded with a loud snap. It turned to a hundred milky fragments that burst inward, showering Meade and Hannah with fine needles of glass. The echo of the high-powered rifle shot followed the breaking glass instantly, the bullet slamming between their faces and exiting through the missing rear window of the truck cab. Meade grabbed Hannah's head and pulled her down to the floor with him. "Are you all right?" he whispered.

"My face . . ."

"It's glass. Don't worry now." Outside all was silent. The wind whistled through the windshield hole and rustled through the broken refrigerators and endless objects in the Trader's yard. Meade looked up from the floor, noticing the angle at which the shot had entered, slightly from Hannah's side of the truck, judging by the warp of the fragments of safety glass that still clung to the frame of the windshield. Whoever had shot would probably approach the truck from that side. The split second between the shattering of the windshield and the sound of the shot, Meade gauged, meant that the shooter had to be a hundred yards away or more. That was what had saved them. Judging from the sound it was a .303 hunting rifle, probably with scope. The distance and the darkness and the wind had combined to make the shot inaccurate.

They didn't have much time. Meade picked a few needle points of glass from his face, not much blood, and could hear Hannah doing the same. She hadn't panicked. He smiled grimly in the darkness. That's one reason he'd come back. The woman simply didn't go shrieky when things happened fast.

Meade quietly opened the driver's door, away from the direction of the shot, and whispered, "No chance for the cars. We'll take the back path to the old man's. Can you make it?"

"Yes," she whispered.

Meade could hear footsteps when he hit the ground, pulling Hannah behind him. Dragging her by the hand he ran silently behind a huge bathtub and crouched. Hannah kneeled beside him, needing no instructions. She was partly a Montana girl and knew how to behave in hunting situations. And this was a hunt. Meade's system was tuned to it, ready for it, his mind alive and calculating, his body ready to make the right move. He was home, on familiar turf, and the rifleman, whoever he was, was not, judging by the stumbling noises and quiet curses. The balance was that Meade was unarmed, fair game in the darkness.

As the footsteps approached the opposite side of the

truck, they could hear the hunter fumble for the fire truck's door handle. Meade tapped Hannah's wrist and they glided off, weaving through the tangle of junk toward the back of the Trader's cabin where an old path led down the hill beside a creek and off over into the next rise, the beginning of a low field that led to the Brigadier's ranch, a half mile distant.

Just as they reached the corner of the shack, Hannah's shin connected painfully with a glass jar which crashed into something else in the tangle of junk, unnaturally loud in the silence. She let out a surprised yelp. Meade jerked her around the corner of the tarpaper building. The shot was surprisingly quick, blowing a chunk of wall out just behind them. And very accurate for an instinct shot, Meade thought quickly. They slid down the creek bank ten yards behind the shack and landed on the broad graveled bank of it. They ran lightly, Meade leading, throwing the lashing beech branches out of their way. They could hear the hunter starting in the direction of the noise.

Meade doubted that it was Gruen on his trail. Gruen wouldn't have shot that way. He didn't know the man as well as he might, but Meade doubted that he'd try a killer shot. He'd rather bring him in. And he couldn't imagine that Gruen would chance injuring an innocent party like Hannah. Also the shot was a gamble, too far, too much wind and darkness. No, Gruen would have made sure and lit him up without risking a miss, if indeed he wanted to shoot. This was someone else. An expert. That second shot was pure instinct.

Meade came to a halt, Hannah bumping into him, the warm length of her body tense. He put his arm around her and her trembling quieted. Her teeth were chattering, her face had a few slivers of glass in it, but her sense of humor was intact. "It's always a real good time to go out with you, Meade. I meet the nicest people," she whispered shakily. The thrashing through the brush was coming closer. The hunter was obviously following the creek, too. And then his sounds stopped. Silence settled down through the high pitch of the wind.

Damn, thought Meade, the bastard is too smart to keep on coming. There was no chance of lying in wait and letting him pass or jumping him. Meade suddenly realized that that was a Nam tactic. Whoever was after them had been over. His thoughts shifted to his father's ranch. He didn't want the old man in jeopardy, but he was a tough old bird. And this was a situation that didn't let anyone off the hook. At the ranch, Billy Sky would be somewhere in the shadows with the .10-gauge. And there were the huskies, Mike and Dan. And a garage full of vehicles. It was his only choice. He moved out slowly with Hannah, calculating how to get across the low field of vetch without being killed from behind, where the hunter could lurk at the edge of the trees and they would be silhouetted against the sky as they went up the rise and across the field toward the ranch house. Footsteps began behind them again.

When they first heard the shots, Dan and Mike, the huskies, began to cast out from the house in the direction of the Trader's shack, working over the field of vetch, noses to the earth, ears alert. It was Dan, the big silver-tipped one, that first caught sight of the two running figures. He crouched low and moved forward in a swift crawl, ready to spring. Mike, the smaller of the two highly trained animals, hung back, walking a wide arc between the house and the running figures, exactly as he had been taught. Meade caught sight of Dan, crawling quickly toward him.

He waited until the dog was almost ready to spring, running hard, Hannah beside him, pounding over the hard surface of the field. He gauged the dog's leap. "Starboard," he hissed, for he didn't want their friend behind him to catch onto the command. The dog rose from its crouch just as it heard Meade's voice, ready then to flop down hard on the dirt and remain motionless. At just that second the .303 slug tore into its wide chest, killing the animal instantly, the velocity of the bullet kicking its body end over end ten feet, where it collapsed lifeless and limp, its jaw working in an after-death spasm of nerve impulses.

Hannah cried out, a single note of despair caught in the cold wind, and they ran on. The next shot kicked up a gout of black soil six inches from Meade's cowboy boot. They neared the safety of the dog pens and the long building to which they were attached. Meade was pacing a flat-out run for the roses, holding back for Hannah, who was surprisingly fast. Even as kids they'd raced each other, and he knew she was swift, but when someone is shooting at you, the adrenaline charges the muscles amazingly. And she hadn't given up when she saw the dog buy it.

They turned the corner of the building, and Meade brought her to a stop. Enough of it, he thought. I'll have to take this guy right now. He held Hannah against the building and carefully stuck his head around the corner. The field was empty. The dead dog lay like a sack of blackness. Nothing moved. The hunter hadn't time to sprint the field. He was still somewhere out there, maybe scared off by the farm and its promise of help, or working his way around the line of windbreak pine trees that led up to the farthest shed.

"Go to the garage," he whispered to Hannah. "Can you do that?"

"Of course," she said.

"Over the tool bench is a shotgun. It should be loaded.

There will be a box of shells in the metal locker on the far side of the garage. Get them and get into the Lincoln. The keys are in the ignition because the old man thinks this place is impregnable. The door-raising button is on the dash near the ignition. If you hear me call, hit the button and get the car out fast." He didn't wait to check this stream of instructions, but took off past her, headed for the shed where the lawn tools were kept on the far side of the farm yard. Hannah was headed for the garage when the yard was suddenly awash in light. The Brigadier was up, his shadow visible at the kitchen door. He stepped out onto the porch, squinting in the shadows.

"Douse the lights!" Meade cried, as he weaved his way toward the tool shed. The Brigadier was a military man and knew his tactics. He quickly ran into the house and the yard went dark again. The old man was no fool. He'd probably be heading toward his impressive gun rack in the study, which took up a whole wall, the way another would have had a Wurlitzer organ proudly displayed. Meade slipped into the small dark tool shed, gingerly worked around the big riding lawn tractor and the neat wall of tools to the small window that looked out on the line of trees that bordered the vetch field. He wished that he was standing before his father's gun rack at that very moment, instead of out here in the cold, empty-handed. Still nothing moved near the edges of the field. His mind worked over the possibilities of the situation. First: Where the hell was Billy Sky? Second: What would the old man do? Meade didn't know the answer to the first question, but he felt sure that the Brigadier would back him up. The actions with the lights were too sure to be mistaken. He was in the house somewhere with a firearm. Third: Had the hunter left off and gone to get help? Maybe he was law, but Meade doubted it. Anybody with half a brain could have taken him in the fire truck. As easily as a baby. If the hunter was headed for help, or waiting for reinforcements, Meade should roar out of there now.

But there were problems, as always. The money. Meade was damned if he was going to leave without it. There was that, that and the fact that he wanted this whole escapade to be clean. The first blood in the whole operation that he'd seen were the three thin trickles of it on Hannah's cheeks where the glass fragments had pricked the skin. Then the dog. That was enough. He wanted out of the farm without another drop spilled. If it came to a choice between blood and the money, Meade thought he knew what he'd choose. Even survival was no excuse. He wanted to go sailing. He'd done enough killing. There shouldn't have to be a choice.

He settled down to watch the field, feeling exposed on the other three sides. Hannah should be in the car by now, probably nervous as hell, and his father in the house and Billy Sky, God knew where. And the hunter could be up to too many tricks. It was not a good position for an efficient getaway, or even a defense. He'd give it five minutes and then go out in the Lincoln with Hannah.

Gruen wheeled the van along the well-lit strip on Missoula's west side, gliding past the bars and car lots and fast-food huts. He'd spent the day staked out near the Brigadier's. His eyes ached from the binoculars. He'd had to stay out of range of the dogs and had been forced to sit in a tree all afternoon across a wheat field from the ranch, watching the place. Nothing had gone on. The Brigadier had fed the dogs just before the early sunset as Gruen sat cramped and chilled in the tree. The old

Indian had gone off in a diseased panel truck with no
fenders shortly after dark, probably for a night in town,
for he was duded up in a white shirt and clean jeans and
had on a new hat.

Gruen had come down from the tree at eight o'clock
and hurried back into town, to eat and check with the
FBI. He probably should have sent an agent out there to
cover for him, but to hell with the Bureau, they looked
at him as a cheap amateur, a bumbler. Maybe he was, at
that. But he wasn't about to give them the satisfaction of
either confirming his idiocy or getting in on a collar. He'd
eaten a roast beef sandwich in the small FBI office in the
basement of the Missoula post office, listening to the wire
tap tapes. Nothing on the Brigadier's phone, just dog
owners calling up to get information. Nothing much on
Hannah's phone, either. Gruen felt uneasy listening in
on the woman. The previous night made him feel an
intimacy that went beyond his job. But it didn't throw
him off Meade's track.

There was a queer note in the call from Hannah's old
high school chum, Tommy Trader. The FBI agent was
bored with the whole thing. He'd left for coffee while
Gruen replayed it. It simply didn't fit.

Gruen checked the Missoula phone book. There was
no listing for Tommy Trader. He'd left his sandwich
half-eaten and gunned the van over to the Missoula
Library. A quick question to the librarian and a quick
flip through the pages of Hannah's high school yearbook
confirmed it. No Tommy Trader existed. It was a code.
That odd voice had to be Meade's, unless Hannah was
messing around with some married guy, which he
doubted.

And they were going to meet at ten tonight somewhere.
But where? Certainly not the high school. He left the
small, quiet library and headed for Hannah's place, hop-

ing at nine-forty-five to catch her still at home. After that he'd check the Brigadier's. Out of town Gruen's truck rolled under the night sky ablaze with stars in the sudden absence of street lights, where they stopped as if at the edge of a cliff.

It came quickly. Most people never could believe that violence was so swift. One moment the night had been a rustle of cold wind and a silence of stars, and the next moment, it was shattered by the sound of a .45 automatic and the crack of a high-velocity rifle. "Shit!" Meade said. He'd picked the wrong side of the ranch to defend. The hunter was around him, inside his perimeter, and from the direction of the sound, inside the house. Billy Sky wouldn't carry a pistol, so Meade surmised that the hunter and his old man were doing the shooting. He ran quickly through the door of the shed, full tilt across the gravel paths and grass of the inner yard to the garage. When he burst through the door, Hannah was at the wheel of the Lincoln.

"Don't start up!" Meade whispered. He came to the driver's door and Hannah handed over the shotgun and the box of shells without being asked. She looked alarmed but not panicky, her wide-set blue eyes questioning. "Sorry I got you into this, Hannah."

"Shut up, Meade. What do we do? Where is he?"

"I think in the house. There may be more shooting. Don't come out of the garage unless I call you. If anyone but me comes through the door, hit the button and take off, don't even look for me. Stay low and pour it on."

"All right," she sighed, and gripped the wheel tightly with one hand, her other hand on the key. "Watch yourself, Meade." Her concern was genuine and Meade's heart melted. But he had to smile at that suburban New Yorker's "watch yourself"; that the self was something that had to be watched. He nodded and went back into the chilly wind and the deep mass of stars that burned above in the black velvet of the night.

No more shots came from the house. Meade slammed home two thick shells into the chambers of the .12-gauge shotgun as he sprinted across the lawn toward the covered porch that ran around three sides of the old Victorian structure. The lights were still out. Just as he reached the perimeter of the yard bounded by a graveled path twenty-five feet from the porch, Mike, the husky, came snarling low out of the shrubs, defending his last object of training, the Brigadier himself. The dog leaped, a low-arced, high-velocity spring, that took him to Meade's chest, his big jaws clacking just below his throat.

"Starboard!" Meade hissed, rapping the dog sharply on the crown of the head with the butt of the shotgun. The dog fell as if shot, lying totally still at his feet, pressed into the ground.

Before he could take a step, Meade was dazzled by the powerful, mercury-vapor yard lights, which sprang to glowing life around him. The kitchen door flew open, and the Brigadier, in bathrobe and pajamas, one shoulder drenched a sickening purple, came unsteadily onto the porch. The barrel of a .303 was laid next to his ear. Meade's heart did not operate. It had been carefully schooled to transfer all emotion to the frontal lobes. Get your ass clear, then cry. That was a prime rule. One that saved lives.

A thin face with razored mustache, surmounted by oiled black hair, was visible, half a head shorter than the Brigadier, peering around the bloody shoulder. "Well, well," said the high-pitched voice, "as I live and breathe, it's Tech Four James Robert Meade. Howdy, man." The light played odd tricks. The shotgun was held against Meade's hip, the barrel pointed at a slight angle upward, the tip pointing toward the voice.

"Who is that?" Play for time, Meade figured, can't risk a shot with the Brigadier as a shield. The dog lay silently behind him, in his shadow. Meade prayed the animal wouldn't be seen. Oh, God, where was Billy Sky?

"It's Tech One, Mason Remson, Sergeant. Now cut the stall shit and put down the piece. Then go get the blushing bride, unless you sent her for help, which would be silly seeing as how your old man is in a compromising situation here. We all need to have a conference."

Meade laid the shotgun carefully in the grass, moving a half-step left to shield Remson's view of the dog. "My wife doubled back to the shack and got her car, Remson. She went for the police."

Mason Remson. Meade remembered him all too clearly. Remson had kicked a woman out of a Huey gunship for not answering questions. She was at least sixty, the scuttlebutt said, and the red-faced, drunken *New York Times* reporter, about nineteen himself, had gotten onto it like it was the whole civil rights movement and Remson got his ass fired. And rightly, too. Morality was a vague subject over there, but there were lines, and Remson had crossed one that Meade thought couldn't be moved an inch.

Meade hadn't bargained on people like Remson. He wanted to pull a "victimless crime" as they called it in police statistics, but he'd forgotten pure, human evil; greed that brooked no compromise. It was an awesome and very real fact.

The Brigadier sagged against the porch railing suddenly, his knees buckling. Remson drove the muzzle of the rifle hard into the Brigadier's mastoid bone. "Tell him to stand up, Meade, or I'll light him up; a round right through the skull, a .303 can make soup against a head."

The Brigadier in World War II and Korea had never been scratched. Not that he'd avoided it, but he'd just bought lucky time. When the window in the house had shattered inward, he'd gotten off a round before the shadowed figure had rolled across the floor and fired at him, jolting him back against the wall. The pain was not what he'd expected from a bullet wound. He'd thought of something sharp and throbbing, but the pain was huge and wide, as if his shoulder had been cut off.

He realized he was in shock, but his mind was clear enough to figure out that the man with the gun was crazy. The Brigadier could also see the dark length of the dog behind his son. Any moment now Billy Sky would come clattering back from town in that old panel truck, the .10-gauge across his lap. He was stopped from those thoughts by a wave of dizziness. The Brigadier stretched up erect at the pressure of the gun muzzle. Remson stepped around his side.

"It's pretty funny sending your old lady for the cops, Meade." His words were slightly slurred, his stance unsteady, Meade noticed. He was either unhinged by the violence, which Meade doubted from Remson's well-known love of it, or he was drunk.

"What the hell's she gonna tell the cops? 'Hey, my husband, the most wanted man in America, is being attacked by a big bad man'?" Remson's laugh ended in a coughing fit that brought color to his pale cheeks. He was an alcoholic. "I think she's hiding around here somewhere, fella, or I shot her. I'll count to ten and then I put a round through the old man's leg unless you get her. In fact we're going to have a long spell of it here. Your old daddy's gonna look like a Swiss cheese before I get out of you where the money is, I bet. You think you're a pretty hard case, but you don't know the half of it, boy."

"You shot her in the field." Meade kept his gaze steady on the muzzle of the rifle, fifteen feet away. He could smell the alcohol from Remson now. Could smell cordite and blood.

"What? Bullshit. I shot a dog."

"No, you missed the dog. My wife got it." The man was drunk enough over that distance with a scope at night. He might buy the story. On the other hand don't give him a chance. And pray for Billy Sky. "Look, Remson, I know your reputation from Nam. And you were good enough to find me, too. That's all there is. I don't want my father hurt, or myself for that matter. I'll take you to the money."

"Bullshit, Meade. You're a fox, man. Don't pull some ancient history on me."

"It's no trick," Meade sighed, half-believing himself. "Look; if I was up to anything, you'd know it. I just don't want anyone hurt. It's gone far enough. My wife's dead." The dog suddenly let out a loud sigh, but Remson seemed not to notice.

"Where's the money?" Remson's focus seemed to wander. The distance was simply too great for Meade to try a rush or to put the dog onto him. He had to get Remson nearer to him and the dog.

"The money's not far, across those hills. There's a dirt track through there. We'll have to take the Jeep. It's in the garage, I'll go get it." Meade whirled around and took a step, just before, as he'd hoped he would, Remson called out, "Halt, goddamn it!" He came around almost in front of the Brigadier, the barrel of the rifle moving around the old man's throat.

"You're not going anywhere without me, man, me and the old fella here. If anything doesn't smell right, and I mean *anything*, Sergeant, the old man's dead. And you're next. I'll turn your carcass in for the reward instead of the money if I have to. You're worth a lot more than you think, man." Meade got ready as Remson dragged the old man down the steps. The Brigadier had gone quite pale from loss of blood, his legs wobbled, but his eyes were clear as he lurched past his tensed and waiting son. His eyes were on the dog. Mike lay, ears up, his head cocked oddly toward the Brigadier, but he didn't move.

"Hey, Remson," Meade said. "I don't know about you, but I need a drink."

"That's a great idea, there, Meade old man." Remson was obviously drunk, Meade could see it at close range, could see the pale, slim hand with its knotty veins on the gun stock and notice the way the blue barrel traveled out from the hand toward his father. With his other hand Remson fumbled in his pocket and brought out a pint bottle of tequila. He shook it without taking his eyes from Meade or the gun from the Brigadier's mastoid bone. The bottle was empty and he pitched it skidding across the lawn.

Meade was ready to play a long shot. A long shot was all that would save them. "There is more in the house, Remson. I know there's some port."

"What did you say, port? Wine?" sneered Remson.

"Sure," Meade said loudly. "Port!" As he yelled the command he stepped quickly to the right and was just in time as the long and muscular body of Mike drove past him and with one grandly excessive leap was at Remson's throat. Meade dove and tackled his father. The old man went down hard in his weakened condition. Meade rolled with him, the old man's legs clasped firmly in his arms, and dragged himself on top of the Brigadier to shield him.

Mike hit Remson in the chest with his massive fore-paws before the drunken ex-trooper had a chance to move, and the dog's powerful jaws bit through his windpipe in an instant. The force of the animal's charge had kicked Remson over backward, and the dog's pent-up fury over its dead mate and the Brigadier's pain could not be contained. Remson tried to scream to Meade to call off the animal but no sound came from his lips, only a warm infusion on the surface of his neck. It was blood from the dog's bite. His larynx was crushed.

Meade rolled over to yell the command for the dog to stop, but the animal bucked and growled on Remson's chest. Suddenly, the .303 still firmly in Remson's grasp, he began to fire. It was on full automatic and the shots chattered into the porch, blowing out windows and tearing chunks of clapboard from the walls. Meade buried his head until the clip had emptied.

The dog stood, still on Remson's chest, panting happily. The form of the man in the half-light lay still. The automatic garage door was open before Meade's ears cleared of the small-arms echoes and he saw the Lincoln's lights switch on and the big silver car rolling toward him. Hannah brought it to a stop right next to him. She was out of the car and around to Meade in an instant. She stopped before him as he rose from the ground. "You son of a bitch, if you want me in on this don't you ever park me away where I can't see you and where I don't know what's going on." She wheeled away from him and knelt by the Brigadier, who raised himself to a sitting position.

"Hello, Hannah." He coughed and grimaced. "I don't think it hit anything that can't be repaired. The bleeding's not bad and I've had a tetanus shot. Get me into the house and be on your way. Those shots will draw some interest."

Hannah was heartened to see that the Brigadier's mind was working clearly. He was also right. People out here in the frontier of civilized America didn't think twice about a shot in the night. That could be someone bagging a porcupine or a raccoon rummaging in the garbage, or even a whiskey-happy cowboy saluting the great spirit of the night. But a whole clip of automatic-arms fire and the locals would think the Chinese were in Missoula, massing for an attack. They might even go so far as to call the police.

The Brigadier stuck out his hand to Meade and Meade helped him up, wincing at the General's gasp of pain. They took him into the kitchen and broke out his big, army-issue first aid kit. The wound was less serious-looking when Hannah had cleaned it, swabbing it with the orange disinfectant. The bullet had passed through the Brigadier's shoulder. He swallowed two pain killers and began a penicillin cycle with self-administered injection. He looked better. Meade brought him a brandy from the den, but the Brigadier waved it away. "Can't while on these pain killers. I'll be all right now, J. R. I just need a good sleep and a few days around the house, and I'll be as good as new."

Hannah had finished tying a sling for the Brigadier's arm. She looked up at Meade. "Have you called an ambulance?"

The old man looked at Meade and then at Hannah.

"What are you two up to?" she said wearily.

"J. R. can't call an ambulance." The Brigadier shifted painfully in the straight-backed Victorian kitchen chair. "If he does, the authorities discover the dead man in the yard. They ask a lot of questions, they get onto J. R.'s trail, they..."

"It doesn't matter," Meade cut in. He swirled the brandy in the snifter and drank it at a gulp. "I'm not going on with it. I didn't want any bloodshed in this operation. Now you're hurt badly, and that scumbag out there is dead.

"Hannah, you stay here with him. Give me an hour in the Jeep and then call the law and an ambulance. I'll be far away by the time they're on to me. Tell them the truth about what happened tonight. This kind of life was all right in Nam, but there's too many people to hurt here."

"How typical of you, Meade." Hannah's temper flared and flashed in her blue eyes. "Start something and then change your mind. You get me to go with you, run around getting shot at, and then all at once you want to call the whole thing off. No more rain checks, Meade."

"She's right." The Brigadier looked slightly glazed from the pain killer, but a pinkness was returning to his cheeks. "Go ahead with Hannah. I don't need the doctor. Billy Sky will be back here any time now. He'll get rid of that body and no one will be the wiser. Take the Lincoln, Meade."

The Brigadier still had an authority that could mobilize troops and command action. Meade wavered for a moment and then came alive, as if from a depressing dream, looking around at the warm yellow glow of the big farm kitchen. "We'll need the Jeep to get the money."

"Take it," waved the Brigadier with his good arm. "And good luck, son."

"Why do you want me to keep doing this?" Meade asked.

"There's several answers to that and all of them are too long. Go." Meade felt like saluting, but he'd spent his allowance on romanticism that night.

Meade and Hannah ran past Remson's body, still lying in the farmyard lights, one arm thrown out as if leading a cheer, and past the Lincoln. Meade scooped up the shotgun. By the time he reached the garage, Hannah was in the driver's seat, the door swinging upward, pulled by the electric motor. He jumped in, and as they pulled out from the garage, they saw two sets of headlights wing onto the long, tree-lined driveway of the farm, traveling at high speed.

"Shit. We've got company. Go the old track across the hill to your place."

The vehicles coming down the road were making an incredible racket.

"One of them is Billy Sky," Hannah said, shifting into four-wheel drive and gunning the engine. "I'd know the sound of that truck anywhere."

"Who's the other one?"

"I don't know."

"Then let's go. No one can hurt the Brigadier with Billy there." Meade turned in the seat and leveled the shotgun at the approaching vehicle. It was impossible to tell whether the Indian's truck was ahead or not, or to guess who was at the wheel of the other one. "Want me to drive?" Meade yelled against the approaching noise.

Hannah popped the clutch and nearly sent Meade flying over the back of the seat, accelerating up the field, headed toward her own cottage on the dirt trail that wound over the low buttes toward the river.

As he came down the driveway in the van Gruen could see the Jeep and two figures in it. He speeded up, partially blinded by the square of the rearview mirror, where bright lights from the panel truck flashed repeatedly. That goddamned Indian back from town, he thought. Gruen was not about to pull over. He could almost taste Meade. That had to be him in the Jeep. Hannah's place had been quiet and the car still missing as it had been that afternoon, and the man who'd tied the knot in that dog leash was now heading up the rise behind the farm at high speed in the Jeep. Gruen's van shot through the farmyard. He saw the man lying like a big store dummy in the yard and the Lincoln with the door open, but his mind filed it for later.

When the back windows of the van disappeared with an ear-splitting boom and the interior of the vehicle became a sandstorm of glass bits, Gruen ducked, but didn't slow down. That Indian and his cannon had nearly taken off the back of the van, but Gruen was betting that the old panel truck couldn't take a ramming. He jammed on the brakes, stiffening his arms against the wheel. The panel truck slammed into him with such force that his chin whipped down onto his sternum, but he didn't feel it.

He threw the van in gear and with a clanking and clattering of pieces of metal, rubber, and chrome he gunned it up the trail. The rearview mirror was shattered, and the rental didn't have West Coast side mirrors, so Gruen didn't know if the Indian was still after him, but he couldn't hear the infernal racket of the old truck.

The lights were out of sight now and Gruen jounced the van to the top of the butte and looked out on a broad expanse of dark wheat. He shut off his motor and his lights, gripping the .38 he'd taken from the glove box. Through the rear window of the van the farmyard was a small square of light down the hill. No one was after him. Left alone, the cold wind rising up the hill and blowing through the open rear windows, where a few shards of glass tinkled to the floor, Gruen felt his scalp prickle. They had to be headed to Hannah's place! The topography of Missoula was clear in his mind, as clear as he used to visualize a piece of Nam real estate. But he couldn't risk either the time or the danger from that Indian with a cannon turning around to dash back through the Brigadier's place. He took off down the hill, driving with the lights out, in the diffused, white moonlight.

They struggled to push the big raft into the slow pool at the side of the strong main current of the Clark Fork. When it was set, Hannah climbed in and ran aft to the big sweeper oar that controlled the ungainly craft in the rough white water of the river. The raft could hold eight tourists in life jackets, gear, food, and beer for a week's trip. With just the two of them and nothing but a shotgun, it was going to ride high and skitter around some, but possibly they could make it. But make it where?

"Meade, where are we . . ."

"Later. Is there a boat hook on board?"

"A what?"

"Oh, shit, a pole with a hook on the end. What do you call them?"

"A peavey pole. Sure. Why?"

"Let's go." Meade jumped into the raft and fumbled around below the rubber gunwale, finally locating the long pole. He pushed the raft back into the swifter stream and almost fell out of the raft when his eyes were blinded by headlights.

A van had come to a stop on the bank of the river twenty yards upstream. The door opened as the current picked up the raft and drew it downstream.

"Stay down," Meade hissed. Hannah sank to her knees on the cold, shifting bottom of the raft. No shots came their way as the raft drifted around a bend and the lights faded from sight.

Gruen! Damn, who else could have followed them this far. Meade's idea of a real good time was to keep a great distance between himself and Gruen. He'd have to think that one over later however.

"Hannah, get over to the windward bank, as tight as you can. Now." The river bank rose five feet above the stream, across a thin line of gravel and tumbled stone. Hannah knew this section of river better than most folks knew their own driveways.

"Beach it here?" She was confused by the suddenness of the command.

"No, just drift down the bank as close in as you can," Meade said quietly as the raft came out of the roar of the deeper channel into the relative quiet of the slower, side stream. As the raft slid along three feet from the graveled bank Meade stood unsteadily in the bow of the craft, holding the boathook and a flashlight. He played the slender beam along the overhanging trees, big beeches and elms that thrust their dark shapes out over the water. Hannah wondered momentarily if he were looking for people in the trees.

Her attention strayed for a moment, and the raft bumped hard against the graveled bottom of the river knocking Meade to his knees. "Christ's sake," he hissed, scrambling back up to his feet and directing the flashlight beam once again at the trees.

Hannah heard the roar of an engine, probably the van that had come into the Brigadier's yard and then followed them to her place. It was headed downstream. From the sound it was on the old trail beside her neighbor's wheat field, which led to the county road where a bridge crossed over the river. It was four miles on the river, maybe two on the road. Whoever it was would beat them to the bridge. She turned to tell Meade this news just in time to see the boathook snare a loop of rope which hung down from a thick, arching elm branch, six feet out from the bank. The small crook of brass at the end of the pole swayed against the loop in the rope, and Hannah shoved the steering oar sideways to brake the raft. The flashlight beam swung wildly away from the drifting pole. The next thing Hannah heard was a thick splash. "Meade! Are you okay?" She heard a chuckle from the bow and Meade said, "Okay, let's get out of here."

Meade dragged the waterproof sack of money on its attached rope into the raft. It had been rigged on the branch with lines ending in loops that snaked out from the tree both over the river and back on the woods twenty feet from the bank. It was done with a spring line, the way one would moor a boat to a dock, to hold the sack taut with the expansions and contractions of the tree and against the wind. Meade had rigged it the night before he'd met Hannah.

In fact, he'd stopped by her place that night, but seeing a strange van had gone on without approaching the cabin in the darkness. A van. Was it the van that chased them? Hannah had said nothing about Gruen being there, and yet she knew who he was. There had hardly been time to discuss the matter. That would be first on the list, when there was time to do more than react. Now the problem was to get away quickly.

"Meade, that truck. It must have gone by us on shore when you pulled that sack out of the tree. There's an old county bridge about a mile away. They could be waiting . . ."

The van splintered the wood farm gate, tires singing over the metal cattle guard that kept livestock from crossing the two-lane blacktop road. Gruen skidded the van, swung it left, and raced for the river. The Clark

Fork was a winding snake of water, and Gruen was sure he'd beaten the raft this far down. He braked quickly in the middle of the narrow, steel bridge. The river disappeared upstream into a tangle of branches and darkness. Gruen gripped the .38. He wished desperately for a rifle. The moon drifted behind a great black puff of cloud and the night went dark. He needed light on that river surface.

He swung the van around sideways on the bridge, but the headlights were twelve feet above the stream, lost in the dimness where they finally contacted the surface of the dark water, far upstream. He backed the van slowly toward the railing behind him. Finally the van's tires came up solid against the base of the bridge. He dug the accelerator harder, and the van bounced up, its back wheels on a narrow cement curb. It was enough to point the headlights downward on the water, the pattern of the woven steel bridge side expanding into great X's of shadow out on the river.

Gruen shut off the lights and the engine. He got out and ran to the railing. He could hear nothing but the whispering wind and the deep rumble of the river working around and over tumbled boulders and logs. He figured the angle. He backed up and stood by the open door of the van, one hand on the headlight switch, and in the other, the pistol.

If Gruen were careful, he could sink the raft. Hannah must know the river well, maybe try to slide by his vantage point somehow, but it looked good for Gruen. A raft that size was compartmented, the air of one section sealed from that of another. He'd helped her repair one. If he could shoot out enough of the compartments, the damn thing would sink, and he'd have Mr. and Mrs. Meade and maybe the money, right where they should be, under the gun.

Gruen's brain flicked over to another scenario, one he didn't like, in which he couldn't shoot the raft, in which he was fired on, or in which he had to shoot at the man on the raft. He dismissed the little picture from his mind.

His eyes strained at the stream, where all he could make out was the shape of the river. Any moment now. He tightened his grip on the pistol. And then it became distinct, a shape drifting on the water. He let the raft come down toward him for another few seconds, until it would be just above his headlights. He would only have a few seconds of illumination before the raft passed beyond his lights.

He hit the switch, ran to the railing, and steadied his three-point shooting stance, his left hand cupping the butt of the gun, and his arms braced over the rail. The raft slid into the lightbeams, a sudden bright orange in the surrounding dark.

It was empty.

There wasn't enough room under the near-side gunwale to lie down and hide. Meade and Hannah had simply disappeared. Gruen stood for a few seconds, still holding the revolver at the ready, as the raft went beyond his lights, quietly under the bridge and down into the waters of the night.

He ran for the truck and tore off, back toward the farm trail. When he swung parallel to the wheat field, heading for Hannah's, Gruen realized that he was smiling. That goddamn Meade was good. What a trick. He simply bailed out of the raft before the bridge.

As he pulled into the cottage yard, the silent dog watched him. Gruen saw that the Jeep was missing. He roared off, following his own tracks back across the butte.

When he pulled into the Brigadier's yard, the Jeep was parked there. The Lincoln that he'd seen earlier was gone. The house was in darkness, and the single all-night yard light, its mercury-vapor brilliance fuzzing off into the edges of the darkness, burned over a secure scene. No dog came out to observe him. Meade could have a gun on him now, but Gruen doubted that. Meade needed running room.

The man he'd seen lying on the ground here a mere half hour ago was gone. Gruen's mind studied the map of highways out of Missoula. He was about to start up the van when the big shotgun muzzle slid through the passenger window. "You fucked up my truck," said Billy Sky.

6
RUNNING ARIZONA

Westfield Monroe felt out of place in Bloomingdale's on a weekday afternoon. Not that he felt exactly comfortable there at any time, but in the middle of the day, when one was supposed to be working, for Christ's sake, it was simply too much. First of all he wasn't dressed for the part. He wore his old tweed jacket with his maroon and white Harvard scarf to ward off the blustery wind of a New York Thanksgiving season. He didn't have a tie on, and he was wearing desert boots. Desert boots had been out of it in New York for at least a decade, but he'd been feeling nostalgic for his college days in Cambridge, and since he had no lunch date, and *Time* magazine writers usually spent the day locked away in their cubicles digesting and rewriting stringer reports, he had no reason to be spiffy. That was early this morning. Now he was in Bloomingdale's, at the important whim of the "Nation" editor, who at the morning meeting had demanded space to do a big feature on this guy

J. R. Meade, "who's captured the imagination of the country. The new Jesse James."

Monroe normally wrote for "Lifestyles," the trendy spot in the magazine where you told a breathless nation about Frisbee-catching dogs or goose-down vests or whatever the latest rage of the week happened to be. His own editor, a chain-smoking menopausal old ironsides called "The Axe," Elinor Spring, had volunteered his services on the J. R. Meade story, because that was exactly what she'd planned for the week anyway, and that was why he was in Bloomingdale's, being stared at by the homosexuals cruising the cologne bar and elegant women on the edge of some expensive hysteria.

In the mish-mash of little counters on the first floor, near the Famous Amos chocolate chip cookie counter, he located what he'd been searching for. The J. R. Meade corner. It was a single glass-topped counter and it held a few surprises. There were J. R. Meade T-shirts, French cotton at $24.95, sporting a silk-screened photo of Meade in a beret from his wanted picture. There was a choice of three legends to accompany the photo: "Stick-em Up," "You'll Never Find Him," and "Why Is This Man Wanted?" They came in several of the latest designer shades. There was also a stack of The Lonesome Cowboys' single, "The Ballad of J. R. Meade," a long mournful dirge about justice and heartbreak and evil "depatees," like a Woody Guthrie/Robin Hood lament of the thirties. There was a new board game called "Chase," in which players moved J. R. Meade cutouts around a board past various road blocks, FBI agents, and through forests. The game included $750,000 of "Meade Money."

The whole counter looked makeshift to Westfield, but amazingly, women in furs, men wearing suits, teens, gays, almost everyone who passed by, stopped to look, and quite a few bought. Westfield scribbled in his notebook for a few moments, getting the thing right. When he saw a break in the action he walked up to the salesgirl.

She was bone thin, her hair dried and teased into a large nest of tiny waves. She wore silver lipstick and had three inch fingernails in a color that must be called owl's blood. She was twenty-two at most, and utterly bored with this blond graduate student standing before her.

"Miss, I'm from *Time* magazine. Working on a story about J. R. Meade."

"Sure." She stared over his shoulder, as if she found the middle distance the most fascinating possibility in a world of infinite choices.

"Are you selling a lot of Meade, uh, stuff?"

"Depends what 'lots' means."

"What kind of people are buying T-shirts for instance?"

"Bloomies."

"What?" Westfield had heard the store called Bloomies, but never its customers.

"Bloomies people," she sighed, as if she'd had to repeat a command to a dog, and turned her back to stack T-shirts in bins. Westfield thought for a moment of stabbing her with his pen, but he was distracted by a woman who'd arrived at the counter.

"Mr. Monroe?" She had a tailored look, obviously managerial.

"Yes?"

"You have a phone call. Your office. You can take it over here." He followed the woman to a wooden desk sporting a vase of fresh-cut flowers. She handed him the phone and swirled away, as if dancing into the endless rows of cosmetics.

"What the hell are you doing in Bloomies in the afternoon. Are you queer?" The Axe could find anyone from Robert Vesco to Jackie O. in half an hour. Even though he'd told no one he was going to the store, he wasn't surprised. In fact if the FBI employed old Elinor, why . . . "Westfield, assuming you're all right and not completely gaga over there, grab a cab to LaGuardia. You're going to Tucson."

"Tucson? Arizona?" New York staffers for *Time* rarely left the building, much less New York. She might as well have said Xanadu. "How long will I be gone? I'll go pack."

"You don't have to bother. I sent a researcher to your apartment. We squared it with your super. She's got a bag and your ticket and your expense money at the American Airlines counter."

"What the hell's the rush? What's the story?"

"J. R. Meade of course. Tomorrow starts a three-day Meade Festival in some damn desert town near Tucson."

"But we should have a stringer there who can . . ."

"We have a *correspondent* there, dear boy. You're going because I've arranged with the Nation editor to give you your big break. Don't blow it, because I don't want you back here in Lifestyles if you hang out at Bloomingdale's. Enough queers here now."

"Goddamn it, Elinor, stop the fag jokes. Why's it so important to the magazine? They don't send people out from New York for this kind of story."

"Look, I'm due in a meeting. In Seattle there's been a riot over J. R. Meade by the blue-collar, ten-four types who love him. One hundred little girls with wet pants from a Kiss concert in Alexandria went to the White House and picketed at midnight with matches for a pardon for him. A group of right-wing businessmen, led by that asshole who owns franchised steak houses, is offering their own reward for him, to preserve the American way of life. Meade is becoming the biggest dividing point since Vietnam in our national consciousness. Now get on it. You know what they want, sights and sounds, whys and wherefores. You're the new Charles Kuralt. And those Mexican boys in Tucson ought to get you off. Your plane leaves in an hour, hot shot."

"Goddamn it, Elinor, Mexican jokes are . . ." The phone buzzed in his ear.

Westfield looked up to see a tall girl in Levis and high boots walking toward him as if going into battle, her mink coat swinging open and her large, well-spaced breasts distorting the wanted picture of J. R. Meade on the purple T-shirt. "Why Is This Man Wanted?" her breasts said. Westfield intended to find out.

Fredonia, Arizona, wasn't much, Gruen thought. Particularly when you were there on a whim. A sad little main street bathed in sunshine but near freezing, with icy winds that blew from the snow-capped mountains all around. Fifty miles south was the Grand Canyon, cold and forlorn this time of year. And far south, after you wound down out of the mountains and reached the heat of the desert floor, after you drove through the scrub and the Seguero cactus that reminded people of old cowboy movies, you drove through Tucson, a city of Mexicans, university students, and some of the rougher elements that came to brown in the sunbelt. Tucson was fifty miles north of Nogales, a jumping off place into the wilds of Sonora, Mexico.

Gruen was operating on a hunch, a feeling that Meade would make a break to Mexico. He sat in Fredonia's McDonald's eating a hamburger that sat like a little corpse in a Styrofoam box. Funny how even in a town that hadn't changed much since the nineteenth century, they could ruin your stomach through the miracle of

modern franchising. The place was full of Indians, Mexicans, and a few of the local whites, stringy, sunburned
folks who chewed their hamburgers as if wringing from
them the last particle of nourishment.

Three days before in Missoula Gruen had decided that
Meade had to head south. That damned Indian had held
him at the Brigadier's half the night, the big shotgun
never straying from him. In the farmhouse kitchen he'd
asked a few questions. The Brigadier was wounded,
seemed to be in shock a bit, but he was able to talk.

No, Gruen was mistaken, the Brigadier said, there'd
been no one lying in the yard. And he'd wounded himself cleaning a gun, but he was all right now. Billy Sky
thought he was a trespasser and so he had detained him.
The Brigadier decided not to call the police, seeing as
how he knew who Gruen was, but still, without a warrant,
he was trespassing on private property.

Gruen closed up the Styrofoam box over the cold
hamburger, half-eaten and lying in its resting place as if
dead. He'd told the Brigadier, as forcefully as he could
with that shotgun resting across the impassive Indian's
knees, that he was detaining an officer of the federal
government, and that it was a federal offense. The Brigadier wasn't too hurt to play his cards just right, with
hesitations and offers to call the FBI.

It was almost dawn before Gruen had gotten out of
there. He wasn't anxious to let the FBI in on it, and the
Brigadier knew that. They'd already written off Missoula,
so why let them know they'd blown it? Of course he was
supposed to keep the Bureau up to date. But what it
came down to was that he admired the Brigadier too
much to put him through the kind of three-act drama the
FBI would stage at the farm. And it wouldn't help catch
Meade. That was what mattered.

Either Gruen had seen the Brigadier lying in the yard

wounded, or it was someone who had no business there. If it had been any lawman, his failure to report in would have caused the place to be swarming with officers by that time. Of course, he thought, the Brigadier could handle just about anything, but calling the Bureau in would mean that Gruen would have to hang around and assist and do just a whole lot of explaining that would eat up time.

He walked outside into the blustery cold of the mountain wind. The north Arizona midmorning sun dazzled through the chill. Gruen climbed into the government motor pool Plymouth and spread the map out against the steering wheel.

Then he'd looked at the map as if Missoula were the center of the universe, and the roads leading out of it were highways to the edge of the world. For a federal agent the world ended at the United States borders. Gruen knew that the closest border was Canada. In an eight-hour drive Meade could have slipped over that dotted line, where Alberta hung like a huge ham in mapmaker pink.

But he wouldn't. Meade was a sailor. A man with a dream to sail. Even though in Vancouver, British Columbia, or on a long run east to Nova Scotia, Meade could arrange a sailboat, the Canadian government was cooperating with the Americans in the hunt for him. Even if Meade weren't aware of that—but he surely would be—he'd been army-trained for avoiding detection.

Canadians spoke English, they were aware of the differences in people, in accents, in cars and clothes. The Canadian coast guard was effective and sharp. They'd spot a strange sailboat perhaps. And the waters of eastern Canada would be rough and freezing cold now. Three strikes against Canada.

At the bottom of the map was the great ocher funnel of Mexico. There a *gringo* was a *gringo*, who could tell the difference? They all looked alike. They spoke a strange language and no one could detect the subtleties of accent. Clothes? These *yanquis* were on vacation. They all dressed funny. The waters of the Gulf of Mexico were warm and the breezes easterly; they would carry a boat under sail out to the Caribbean with an easy reach. The patrols of the Mexican government were spotty, relaxed, and of not much use. If Gruen were going to go sailing, he'd certainly pick Mexico over Canada. But Meade was a wily character. He'd figure the odds on what the opposition might decide and try to throw them off.

Gruen also dismissed the American coastlines. Too many chances of being discovered. Meade was a media hero now. Some guy from *Sixty Minutes* kept calling Gruen's Seattle office. A *Time* reporter was also trying to get him. Everywhere he went these past three days he'd seen Meade all over the papers or on television, or T-shirts, posters, even bumper stickers that said "Meade Lives!" That was a response to the FBI's half-assed theory, which they pushed everywhere, that Meade died in the jump into the woods and it was just a matter of time before they would find his remains. All that had done was to fill the Pinchot National Forest with every kind of useless speculator, unemployed brick layer, and long-shot artist in the country. It was a hell of a mess up there, according to the home office.

Gruen folded away his map. There was only one way south from Fredonia, along Route 89 past the east rim of the Grand Canyon down through Flagstaff and into the desert. It had to be Mexico, there was no other choice.

Gruen swung out onto the nearly deserted main street, heading for the rim of the Canyon. How the hell to find Meade was the question. It would absorb him on the long

drive to Tucson. One thing was sure: Meade didn't mix
with crowds. He'd stay off the interstates and stick to the
rural ways. And those were the routes Gruen would
travel.

On the front of the yellow T-shirt the man wore, the
legend read "South Rim Feed and Grain Co." He stood
in the batter's box and belched, a long, low blast as he
stared into the distance.

"Jesus," said Meade, wiping beer foam from his newly
sprouted mustache, "that whole team is drunk." The
batter swung mightily at the slow-pitched softball as it
looped over the plate. He connected for a bouncing
single, which turned into a stand-up double when the
first baseman of the A & P Tigers missed the throw and
wandered off to retrieve a can of beer from a tub of ice
at one side of the field.

"When you took off the last time, I played on a
women's team in Missoula, Meade. Did you know that?"
Hannah drank from her own can of beer. It was a warm-
ish evening sitting in the bleachers outside the town of
Flagstaff, Arizona. Although Christmas was only two
weeks away, the softball league was apparently in full
swing. A few wives and friends of the team members sat
in the bleachers, hollering and laughing. When Hannah
had seen the game from the highway, she'd asked Meade
to stop and see a few innings. They'd bought a six-pack
of beer, a sack of Fritos, and some cheese at a grocery
across the street and relaxed for a while.

The runner who'd been on first tried to steal second
while the pitcher was drinking beer, but he got tagged
hard on the head by the second baseman and a fight
began, more of a wrestling match really, both men too
drunk and too uninspired to be serious.

"You know, before my mother died, she'd never let me do anything athletic. She was always afraid I'd get huge biceps and calves. It was a weird idea." Hannah smiled.

Meade looked at her appraisingly. "My old man had an 'idea' about me, too. I don't think he saw much of me. He mostly saw the idea."

"What was his idea? Oh, Christ, they're useless." Hannah watched the two teams trying to break up the fight. "The Brigadier's all right, you know."

"Sure, Hannah, he's okay. But you don't see that when you're fourteen and the smartest asshole that ever lived."

Hannah grabbed Meade's hand and held it tightly. "And now you're a grown-up asshole? Huh?"

Meade laughed and pinched her on the thigh. He realized that his laughter had become a rare sound, lately. It was pleasant to sit with Hannah, feeling her strength and warmth through her quick intelligence on a fine evening in Arizona. For all of ten minutes Meade had forgotten to check out every single soul looking at him. It was almost dark, and their new disguises should work here in the shadows of sunset.

Meade wore a plaid shirt and a pair of those backpackers' corduroys with pockets all over them and hiking boots. With the mustache and the addition of horn-rim glasses and an Irish tweed hat, he looked like a serious backpacker. And in the old Chevy parked at the curb were two very professional pack frames and other gear. Hannah was dressed similarly. Suddenly Meade remembered that he had wanted to find out something from Hannah. "You know I was in Missoula the night before I called you."

Hannah watched the game, which had started up again after the two battlers had been sidelined with a pint of whiskey as a consolation prize. "Oh, yeah?"

"I was hiding the money down by your place. And I

stopped to look around your cabin, but there was a strange van parked there so I didn't dare come in."

"Oh, yeah, that was that Gruen guy." Hannah studied the field very closely, as if softball were a religious experience that had to be paid close attention.

"What did he want?"

"What everybody wanted the last few weeks, Meade, your ass on a platter." She sucked at her beer.

"That's all, huh?"

"You know, Meade, there's this gal, Shirley, that played softball with me. When her husband took off last spring and was gone for a week, she put all his clothes and stuff in big green trash bags out on the porch and locked the doors. A few days later the bags were gone. Shirley never saw him again."

"All right, goddamnit. You don't have to give me parables. It's none of my business, right?"

"That's right. But just for the record, I had a few offers and some of those I thought over. But I didn't take anybody up on it." Hannah smiled and flashed her eyes at Meade. "Maybe I should have when I had the chance, though. 'Cause it looks like I'm stuck with you from now on."

"Tough shit." Meade held her hand and looked at the softball game in the gathering dusk. The shadows and the darkness would protect him from being recognized, and protect him from Hannah seeing the tears that blurred his eyes for a moment. Being in love was a pain in the ass sometimes, when you should be keeping your mind on business.

The desert was cold at night. Meade had pitched the small, red backpacks near a pillar of rock left from the

time the desert was the ocean floor, and had built a small
campfire. The beer from the evening was gone, and he'd
put on a pot of coffee. It was a quiet locale, halfway
down the Rockies into the Sonoran desert, where Phoenix
and Tucson lay. On the old side road nearby an occasional truck or Jeep ground by.

Meade sat close to the fire, where the coffeepot hung
from a spit, warming. He held a tin cup of the liquid,
reading the day-old paper that they'd picked up earlier
at a twenty-four-hour truck stop. The editorial, entitled
"Felons Into Heroes—The Broken Dream," made him
smile. It concluded ". . . how J. R. Meade has become a
hero to the young is not as important as the fact itself.
Something is seriously wrong with this country of ours
when drug-addict rock stars and common thieves are the
models which our young people admire. A nation of
J. R. Meades is a frightening and real possibility, one
that we must guard against by holding up to our youth
more enduring models of admiration. This is a job of
the schools, parents, the government, everyone. And it
is a job we'd better get busy with right now."

"Amen," said Meade, tossing the paper aside. "A
nation of J. R. Meades. Jesus Christ."

"What did you say?" Hannah crawled out of the circular opening of the small tent, a feat for a contortionist.
"Why the hell couldn't we get a tent that had a normal
doorway, Meade? And why are you out here talking to
yourself?"

"The paper says that America could become a nation
of J. R. Meades. And we can't have a normal tent like
regular folks, because we're not regular folks, we're concerned environmentalists who normally go backpacking,
but we're driving down to Mexico first and then walking
through Sonora for a month. So we've got a backpacking
tent. We're just a couple of good-living people who want

to walk through Mexico for the spiritual uplift of it, Hannah."

She stretched, bent to get some coffee from the pot over the fire, filling Meade with an ache of lust. She sat by him, sipping coffee, her hair tied back with a blue bandana. "That goddamn dehydrated food will make us old before our time, Meade. I never carried that crap on raft trips. I couldn't feed it to paying customers."

Meade put an arm around her waist and drew her hip over against his own. He could feel her warmth through their clothing, in the chilly pool of shadow. "Well, you know how it is with us backpackers, we're feeding our souls on the quiet beauty of the wilderness, we don't care about how the body fares. Except I sure care about how your body fares, ma'am." Meade ran his hand over her hips.

"You've certainly proved that over the last few days. But doing it in the back of the car by the road was a bit much, Meade. You really think you're a kid, don't you?"

"Got to live the part, or someone will see through the disguise." Meade smiled and drank coffee.

Hannah thought that she'd never seen him so content as he was at that moment. In fact since they'd started running three days before Meade was like a different person. This wasn't the Meade who had mooned around the place after Vietnam, nor the Meade who'd read sailing books before the army. This was a man in charge of himself and his destiny. For a change Meade was a pleasure to be with.

"Meade, why the hell are you so happy? Every cop in the country is looking for you, and you're running around putting on disguises like it was all a grand joke. I want to get to Mexico and get out of all this, but I swear that you're prolonging it. I just want to know why."

Meade stared out at the desert, so different from Viet-

nam. But the feeling was similar. "I'm not trying to pro-
long it, Hannah. It's just that being on the move, being
alert to danger is a kind of life for me.

"I was riding a Huey gunship in Nam once, when I
first got over there. They're helicopters fitted with more
armament than you could imagine. The crew was young.
Hell, a couple of them still had pimples. And they were
all stoned to the eyeballs on Tai sticks. We were flying
low over the jungle, way in by the Cambodian border.
We came over a clearing where a herd of elephants were
stripping leaves from trees. They're little beasts over
there, compared to the circus ones anyway. Intelligent
animals. They looked up at the chopper, quite curious.

"And this little stoned gunner never said a word, he
just fitted himself into a shoulder harness of the machine
gun and shot at them. Most of them got into the trees
quickly, but the gunner hit one. The elephant tipped
over on its side, blood everywhere. The damned pilot
never said anything either, he circled the clearing so that
the gunner could destroy that animal. I didn't say anything, no one mentioned it afterward. But I couldn't
forget the look in that elephant's eyes before it died. It
was looking up at the helicopter wondering what the
hell had happened to it. The gunner emptied a whole
belt of ammunition into it. It was the saddest thing I've
ever seen. I didn't understand it anymore than the
elephant.

"I want to stay alive, Hannah, and I've learned that I've
always been pursued. The army, my father, my own
dreams. So I like to be ready for anything. It makes me
feel, I guess, more alive."

Hannah pulled away from Meade's shoulder and
looked into his eyes. "But you don't have to steal a lot
of money and have the whole damn country looking for
you to feel more 'alive,' do you?"

Meade laughed and flopped over on his back staring up at the deep blue of the desert sky. "No. That was my own way to *stay* alive, to feel it. And besides it gives the bastards something to do. And me too."

"And now we sail around the world?"

Meade rolled over and pulled her down in the sandy soil beside him, threw his leg over her and kissed her hard. She laced her arms around his neck. "We sail around the world three or four times," he murmured.

"And then what, Meade?"

"Then we hit another airline if we have to." He kissed her again. Hannah drew back from Meade and looked frightened suddenly, as if a shadow had passed over her heart.

"They'd stop, wouldn't they, if you gave the money back?"

Meade held her tightly. "No," he whispered, "they'd keep coming. In fact it would piss them off. There's no way to stop them, Hannah, just get away from them. That's the trick." His lips pressed against her own, and she opened her mouth to him with a hunger that surprised him.

Hannah was buttoning up her plaid shirt and Meade was pouring coffee when they both heard the distinctive click of a pistol being cocked. "Don't do anything dumb. Just stand still." The voice sounded to Meade like it had some seasoning in it, age perhaps. It was a man's voice, gravelly and wily.

"Walk over next to the girl, fella." Meade did as he was ordered, able to glimpse from his peripheral vision a strange-looking figure. "All right, turn around and let's have a look at you."

The man was in his sixties, his gray hair wild and

windblown, and he needed a shave, could have used one
three days ago at least. He had a round face, small veins
in traces of purple working over the weathered surface
of his cheeks. But the most amazing thing about him was
the coat he wore. It was a shiny gray material, thick and
quilted. It extended from a standup collar which bumped
his chin to his ankles. He resembled something out of a
bad science fiction movie. In his hand was a .44 magnum
Rugger. A cannon of a pistol, so powerful Meade shuddered inside. Where had this hairy old bastard come
from? Even when making love Meade kept an ear open,
or so he thought. He wasn't worried so much about dying
as he was suffering from embarrassment. Nailed by some
old desert rat. Meade's pride was suffering. And Hannah
must be embarrassed too, Meade thought, wondering if
the old man had seen them making love.

"How long have you been here?" she asked, hands on
her hips.

The old man scratched his chin, the gun steady in his
hand. "Just long enough to decide that you're the right
ones."

"The ones what?" asked Meade, calculating the distance from the barrel of the Rugger to his heart. The
old man shambled toward them, coming very close to
Meade. Meade decided that he wasn't going to die. He
was about to lunge sideways and down, hoping that the
old man's reflexes weren't as fast as his own. But the
gray-haired apparition turned the .44 around in his hand
and handed it to Meade. He turned his back and paced
off ten yards and whirled again in the huge, metallic coat.

"I decided that you're the one that's going to shoot me.
I don't have much choice anyway. Nobody else around
here. Now shoot right for the middle of my chest." The
old man shut his eyes and flung out his arms, offering
his body up to fate.

Meade quickly pointed the .44 at the ground. "What

the hell are you talking about, fella? This is a .44 magnum, it'd blow you clear across the desert."

"Oh, no it won't, young fella. I am wearing the first,
genuine Walk Softly coat and nothing, I mean nothing,
can get through it. Now this is the final test. What the
hell do you care? It's my invention and it'll work."

"Where did you come from?" Hannah was as astonished as Meade. The old man stood with his arms straight
out.

"I come from where we all return. Now shoot, you
chickenshit son of a bitch."

"Hey, hey, calm down, old man," Meade said gently.
He was crazy or drunk, or he'd been in the desert too
long.

"No need to be calm. I'm going to be calm a long
time after I'm dead, young man. I've got incurable cancer
of the bowel. This coat is my gift to the world. Let an
old man be proud of himself one last time. I've worked
perfecting the coat for ten years, and it's my legacy. Now
prove it for me. If it fails, what the hell. It'll just save
me a long death in a hospital." The old man's chin jutted
out toward Meade with a splendid defiance, the wattles
of his neck shaking with emotion.

Meade recognized something in the man's speech, some
shred of a dream that had driven Meade himself. This
old fella was laying it on the line. Out here playing
pranks at his age. Meade felt a kinship with this red-eyed
old loon, standing there like a padded, aged Christ with
his arms out in benediction to the empty wastes of the
desert.

"Meade, oh, my God! Don't!" Hannah screamed. The
pistol in Meade's hand had swung up in an arc and the
barrel pointed dead level with the old man's chest.
"Stop!"

The pistol went off, a tremendous thunderclap of

sound; shock waves ripped across the desert floor. The old man was lifted up and backward. He flew five feet through the air and landed on his rear end. Sending up a puff of dust. He fell backward, his eyes closed.

"My God, what have you done?" Hannah ran to the man and fell on her knees by his side. Meade looked at the Rugger. The old bastard had filed the trigger down to a hair. Meade was lucky he hadn't shot himself just holding the thing. He didn't know that he was going to shoot. He was confused and full of an unshakable sorrow.

"Ooohh." The old man stirred. He got up on one elbow. Hannah crawled back from him, as if he'd returned from the dead. He shook his head and looked around. His bleary eyes lit on Meade and he smiled. "I lied to you," he coughed. "Oh, boy, sore ribs."

"What did you lie about?" asked Meade astonished.

"I don't have cancer. Sound as a dollar." He sat up, rubbing his chest. "Just had to convince you that you couldn't do any harm to shoot. I'm not crazy. I'm not even dumb. I tested that coat with the .44 twice before. Just not on a person. Wanted to see how it felt to take the force of it. This coat's gonna make my fortune, pal."

Meade began to laugh. The old man grinned, cackled, and fell back on the ground, holding his sore ribs and laughing crazily at the sky. Hannah looked at them both. Two idiots out here in the middle of the desert firing guns and defying death and laughing. She went back and sat by the fire, which burned low, shivered, and rubbed her arms briskly.

"I think we all could use a drink, don't you?" said the old man.

"What's your name?" Meade asked, still wiping his eyes from laughter.

"Elijah Santini; my mother was Jewish and my father was Sicilian. How's that for a mix?"

"I'm Earl Ballard and this is the little woman, Evie," Meade smiled.

"Evie?" Hannah muttered. "You bastard."

"Well, come on, it's only about a mile to my van." The old man, the coat flapping about him, wheeled and stalked off across the desert toward the nearest pillar of rocks, a good mile in the distance. Meade and Hannah followed, Meade still wondering how the old buzzard had managed to find them and sneak up.

Gruen had exhausted his logic on the drive to Flagstaff. His mind was dull and his eye inattentive as he drove into the outskirts of the town which was the jumping-off place for the Grand Canyon. He was searching for a motel, another Travel Lodge or Ramada Inn, one of a seemingly endless line of neutral bedrooms in which he'd slept fitfully the past few nights, his dreams a replay of empty rafts, bodies that disappeared, Indians with shotguns, and dogs that guarded empty yards.

He was two blocks past the dog when it hit home. He cut the car left, an auto behind him screeching to a halt with a sound of brakes and blaring horn. Gruen took no notice of the irate driver shaking his fist as he took a U-turn and raced back, his mind alert and his body alive again.

In the gravel expanse of a used-car lot, one of those second-rate places with rows of plastic propellers strung in the air, where the prices of the junky autos and pickups were painted large on their windshields, was a stand in one corner displaying SPECIAL! SPECIAL! SPECIAL! It was a clean, shining silver Jeep with Montana plates. Near it sat a pale-eyed husky. Silent, staring into the distance. Gruen parked across the street, his heart beating with a wild elation.

It had to be one of those dogs of Meade's! He smacked his hand hard on the steering wheel. He was on to it, now, by God, the hunch was right. Meade was headed toward Mexico, he knew it. He got out and hurried across the street, searching the windows of the small shack in the middle of the lot for a sign of life. The dog watched him, alert.

Elijah Santini sat at the small, neat table in the van, eating a bagel and drinking from a crystal goblet of Chianti. Meade and Hannah sat across from him, each with a glass of wine. While they sipped, Elijah gulped and kept refilling his own glass, flushed with enthusiasm. The interior of the van was something that one could not have predicted from the outside. It was a stock Dodge van, which bore the simple legend SANTINI PIZZA, DETROIT, MICHIGAN. Inside, the cockpit (that was the best word for it) contained every gadget one could imagine. There were radar detectors, digital gas-consumption readout, eight-track/FM stereo, tooled-leather high-back lounge chairs, and the usual high-priced electric doodads. Behind the driver's and passengers' chairs things got even wilder. The floor, walls, and ceiling were covered in chartreuse shag carpeting. Next to the built-in breakfast booth was a stainless-steel galley with sink, two-burner propane stove, and a small refrigerator. Across the rear of the van was a bed covered in fur. Indirect lighting completed the scene and a Sergio Franchi record crooned softly from the speakers. The air conditioning hummed.

"Seven years ago I went out on a call to the north side of Detroit. You see," he said between mouthfuls of wine and bites of bagel, "anyone can make pizza once they know the recipe, but delivering it in a city like Detroit is a real challenge. The call was for a large pie with peppers and mushrooms—and I drove over to the address in a city project apartment. Well, I knock on the door . . ." Elijah, minus the Walk Softly coat, jumped up, crouching under the van ceiling, and acted out his story, his wisps of gray hair blowing in the air conditioning, ". . . and this guy pulls it open and grabs me by the collar, shoves a pistol right up against my head. There were two of them. They took all my money, which was a lot because it was near the end of the night, a Saturday, and then they walloped the shit out of me." Elijah staggered around the van, pummeling himself. Hannah hid her smile behind her wine glass.

"Did you report it to the police?" Meade asked.

The old man stopped hitting himself. "Sure, but in Detroit they're busy with multiple murders and such. Also it could have been cops who held me up." He roared with laughter. "That's the trouble with this country. You've got to protect yourself, take care of your own. No one can do it for you anymore, there's no help."

"I'll drink to that," whispered Meade, sipping his Chianti.

"So I started on the coat. I knew there was an answer in Teflon cloth. I picked up some old army flak jackets and covered them with my wife's Teflon ironing-board cover. It took seven years, but I've got a product that would let you walk through a riot without a scratch."

"What are you doing out here in Arizona, Elijah?" Meade asked.

"Well, down in Tucson there's a law enforcement convention, where all the local cops get together and whine that the courts have tied their hands. I'm going to go see them and sell this coat all over the country. Once the cops try it, hell, I'll try it for them, with that little demonstration that we put on, they'll buy them like there's no tomorrow." The old man ran his spotted, wrinkled hand through his thin hair and drank deeply from the goblet of wine. He flopped back down on the bench behind the table and stared at his hand.

"The bastards called up almost seven years to the day. Peppers and mushrooms. Same address. Except this time I went in the Walk Softly coat and this little beauty." Elijah sleepily waved the .44 and Meade gently took it from him. "And I knocked on the door again and the bastard opened it, but this time I put the .44 right into that creep's snot locker and backed him into the room. His partner had a little Saturday-night special, and he fired the whole cylinder at me, of course I just smiled at them. You should have seen those two boys, their eyes were about to fall out. I was Superman. Scared the shit right out of them. I took them to the nearest precinct and they gave the cops a full confession. Of course they were out on bail the next morning, but they never bothered me again."

"Elijah, those cops you're going to see down in Tucson are pretty cagey old boys. They've got budgets and suppliers who give kickbacks, and they are the kind of people who don't really go for the new things. They're pretty traditional. I wouldn't put too much hope in the Walk Softly coat being a big seller," Meade said gently.

The old man's eyes were only half open now. "Trouble is, young man, I've got about fifty dollars left to my name. Oh, I know it's a dream, but who the hell wants to end up with the fact that their whole life they smelled like garlic? I don't even like pizza. If the cops don't buy, I'll have to sell the van and go home. And you don't know how much I don't want to do that."

The old man fell asleep, his head dropping onto his chest and his body slumping sideways into the carpeted wall of the van. Meade looked at him and thought of the

times in Nam when he'd started to run, when he knew
that there was something more than smelling like garlic
all your life. He and old Elijah were kindred spirits. I'm
hardly a desert prophet, but I have a mission: Don't get
caught with your pants down and don't end up with
nothing to show for your life. It was strange that these
were such painful and difficult lessons to learn, Meade
thought. He tapped Hannah on the arm and they tip-
toed to the door of the van, the old man deep into a
winey sleep, his face flushed but peaceful.

"Is that you when you're old?" Hannah whispered to
Meade.

"There's worse, Hannah." Meade took a wad of money
from the pocket of his backpackers pants. He counted
out five hundred dollars and slipped it onto the driver's
seat of the van.

By the time Gruen hit the low, sunwashed outskirts
of Phoenix, his elation had settled into quiet planning.
The sun dazzled and baked the land, buildings, and
people. The government Plymouth wasn't air condi-
tioned and Gruen drove with all the windows open, past
the sudden lush oases of golf courses, the endless adobe
restaurants and shopping centers. Everywhere the aged
sat on bus-stop benches or rode big-wheeled tricycles,
their watery eyes alert for impending death, their skin as
wrinkled and hoary as tortoises under their dark tans.
Their heads followed the traffic streaming by as slowly
as if they were underwater. Gruen suddenly heard himself say "Thank God" out loud as he waited at a traffic
light.

Thank God for what? For not being one of them. Yet.
Maybe he would never be. The word "retirement"

loomed before him as the light changed to green and he accelerated down the burning road deeper into the megalopolis where illusion was better than death, where the hospital room in which the cancer patient spent his last days was painted a pastel color and the sunshine streamed in like a spring morning back in New Hampshire.

He gripped the hot steering wheel and forced his mind back to business. The used-car dealer in Flagstaff had been an honest man, despite his business. Yes, a man and a woman who looked like tourists had stopped and traded their Jeep on a six-year-old Chevy. They were low on money, they'd said. They had a magnificent dog with them, the husky that sat out front. The woman had cried, but the man had persuaded her that they couldn't take the dog with them to Los Angeles. Man's name was Jim Hawkins, said so on his license. The man had completed the forms for them, and he gave Gruen the description of the Chevrolet.

After Gruen had passed the first telephone booth, where he should have stopped and called both the FAA and the FBI, he felt less guilty. To hell with them. Meade was his case. They'd just muck it up. If you wanted to catch a master at evasion, you didn't take an army with you, you went in alone.

Gruen stopped in a Denny's restaurant, all cantilevered ceilings and plate glass, and ate a hamburger covered with chili, while he read the *Phoenix Sun*. In the entertainment section a full-page article, "Cowpokes Honor Skyjacker," caught his eye. A western music group called The Lonesome Cowboys, famous locally in Phoenix, so it seemed, were hosting a "J. R. Meade Festival" in a ghost town outside of Tucson called Oracle. It was going to be a three-day affair—Friday, Saturday, and Sunday. Beer, chili, and surprise performers. Thousands of young people from out of state were reportedly on their way to Oracle, and one could only guess how many local folks would show up. The Lonesome Cowboys had become instantly rich, the article said, for their recording of "The Ballad of J. R. Meade." They wanted to pay back the folks who bought the record. The beer would be free. And the leader of the group, somebody called Davey, said, "J. R. Meade is cordially invited if he happens to hear about this. He's the man who showed us how to deal with the system."

The group's album, *Running the Money*, was on top of the charts.

Gruen left the hamburger and went to the pay phone by the door to the restrooms. He called the office in Seattle. "I'm going on down to the border for a few days. No sign of Meade. I guess my hunch didn't pay off. But since I'm almost down there anyway, I'll check with the Nogales office and try to round up the reports on the small-aircraft marijuana traffic. We've had enough trouble with them lately, maybe I'll learn something new."

The voice of his district supervisor, a crusty old bureaucrat named Arthur Meyers, crackled over the line. "Gruen, I don't know what the hell you think you're doing. You've got a national clearance to go after Meade because you know him. But if you've lost him, then get back here. There's work to do. There's some sort of riot going on out in the desert out there, and the FBI is going to be all over the place, they've got the border covered like the Berlin Wall. So just get back up here, will you?"

Gruen hung up the phone, paid, and walked out of the restaurant without finishing his meal. On the road to Tucson he figured the odds. J. R. Meade was a careful man, a smart one. But a man who just wanted money, even a lot of it, didn't skyjack a plane, bail out in a parachute, and cause the whole country to go looking for him. There was a bit of the showman in Meade. Gruen remembered him in Vietnam after Meade had escaped from the VC on that long run. He'd started wearing tailored fatigues like the Black Marines did. He had a certain flair. If the bastard was making a run for the border, what better cover for a day than to attend a festival in his own honor. It was a Meade trick, by God, totally unexpected. The car dealer said that the man had talked about going to L.A. Pure cover.

Gruen pulled off the road and studied the map. It took only a minute to find Oracle.

7
THE FESTIVAL

"Oracle is a vast sun-baked dry stretch of desert that ends in a series of exhausted gullies on three sides, but on a recent Friday afternoon, the entire area was converted into one of the largest parking lots in the Southwest," Westfield Monroe scribbled in his notebook. A droplet of perspiration slid from the tip of his nose onto the page and fuzzed out the ink, like a Rorschach test. In a sweat-soaked tennis shirt and khaki shorts Westfield stood on a slight rise between Route 77 and the vast, natural bowl that formed the desert floor outside of Oracle. All Friday morning cars and pickup trucks, campers and trailers had been arriving. A two-engine Cessna from L.A. brought rock music and movie folks. A few limousines had pulled in among the dusty vehicles. The J. R. Meade festival was becoming a scene for the fast set as well as a hoedown for values Westfield thought long gone. These people thought Meade was a hero from the age of outlaws and train robbers.

Westfield trudged up the rise with the L.A. photographer *Time* had sent out to shoot the story, so that the two of them could get an overview of what promised to be a full-scale happening in the desert. The photographer, a gaunt, bearded man in Gucci loafers, Levis, and no shirt, had had his first noseful of cocaine earlier that morning at their motel in Tucson, and he sniffed mightily all the while, talking nonstop. Westfield was tired of it and tucked his notebook into his shorts pocket. "I've got to get down there and mix it up, Will. See you later."

The photographer's wild face appeared around the edge of his Nikon. "All right, writer man, I've got to do another roll of overview up here. Can't tell what the hell they'll want in New York. Catch you down at ringside."

On the long trek back down into the natural arroyo formed by the desert hills Westfield noticed the FBI for the first time. He'd seen the cops, of course, in riot helmets and carrying night sticks to control what looked like could become an ugly crowd if the free beer held out. The cop cars were from Tucson, Phoenix, and points in between. The FBI was more circumspect, but Westfield could spot the agents. They were the ones wearing small, flesh-colored buttons in their ears, sunglasses, and Windbreakers. Who the hell but an FBI agent would wear a Windbreaker when it was ninety degrees?

The band, The Lonesome Cowboys, were tuning up on a flatbed truck in the middle of a sea of human forms, most of whom were stripped to the waist, even many of the girls. There were hundreds of what Westfield could only describe as rednecks: tough-looking men and women, wearing straw cowboy hats and Levis, already well into the big kegs of Lone Star Beer, which were lined up outside several canvas-covered booths like rows of bombs. And there were just as many Southwestern hippies, who also wore cowboy boots and Levis, but instead of cowboy hats wore long, flowing hair and bushy beards. And of course there was the swift set, already provided with folding deck chairs and drinks. As he approached the mass of flesh in the sunshine, the band struck up the chords of "The Ballad of J. R. Meade" and the crowd erupted in a wild roar, spilling beer, setting off firecrackers, waving hats and bras. One girl, her bare breasts swinging in time to the country twang, rode the shoulders of a strapping Indian boy inhaling the largest joint Westfield had ever seen.

The band sang:

> Oh, he took the airline's money
> On Thanksgiving Day,
> He said "This country's kinda funny,"
> and parachuted away.
>
> It's a crazy and strange place,
> and it doesn't make much sense,
> you need a rifle and a shotgun
> just to get on over the fence.
>
> Oh, J. R. Meade is running,
> and the deputy's hunting him down
> with a sack of cash and an M-16
> will he ever get to the ground?

The sound lashed out from large speakers towering at each side of the truck. A CBS crew was shooting with a lightweight camera. It was a certified media event. Westfield grinned. The music was infectious, making him tap his foot, and the crowd undulated in time with the song as it boomed out across the desert.

The police stood nervously, smoking, watching the crowd for signs of trouble, swinging their nightsticks in time with the music. Westfield jumped when he felt a poke in the kidney. He turned to see a wild-looking old man with white hair wearing the strangest coat he'd ever seen.

"You a law enforcement officer, young man? You look like you're watching instead of enjoying. Keeping an eye out for the man himself, huh? You really think he'd be stupid enough to show up here?"

"Uh, I'm a reporter. The cops are all around here. What are you looking for?" Westfield couldn't resist his news instinct. This guy might make a great sidebar. The old man looked him over, trying to peek at what was written in his notebook. "What paper do you work for?" he cackled.

"*Time* magazine."

The old man smiled broadly and put his arm around Westfield. He smelled of wine. "Well, I want to tell you a story, young man, about a dream and a pizza delivery . . ."

Gruen walked into the crowd below the bandstand. He'd never been to a rock concert before, or any young people's happening—unless you'd call Vietnam a happening, where all the scared faces had acne, and there was considerably more dope than this crew seemed able to come up with. Gruen didn't know what he'd find. Another hunch. His string of luck may have played out, but he'd bet Meade would show up. The man had a streak of vanity in his own prowess. He couldn't pass this up. Gruen pushed his way through the bodies packed around the bandstand, working his way to the back, where he could climb the long hill up from the desert floor to get some kind of view of the shape of this gathering, checking the topography, and try to figure where

Meade would plant himself and how he'd take off if necessary.

Pushing past a knot of shirtless young men Gruen stepped on a booted foot. "Excuse me," he murmured.

"Watch that, man." A big, heavily-muscled Texan with a scar running from the gold earring in his left earlobe to the point of his chin turned a grizzled, beer-addled face to Gruen. He put a huge hand on Gruen's arm. "You a cop, fella?" The guy was smiling, his words shouted above the booming base of the speakers as "The Ballad of J. R. Meade" drove to its conclusion. The fellow's buddies turned and cast amused glances at Gruen.

There was simply no need to say anything. Gruen took the advice of an old sergeant who'd been in the service long before Pearl Harbor, when regular army meant tough men. "If trouble starts, move in fast and finish it. Don't talk," he'd told young Private Gruen long ago on Guadalcanal. And Gruen always did just that.

He drove his heel down hard on the cowboy's instep, watching the bleary eyes contract in pain. The cowboy drew back his arm, balling his fist, but Gruen moved in very close to him and jabbed his stiff fingers up under the man's diaphragm. The big figure crumpled without a sound, still clutching his beer cup. Gruen looked evenly at the fellow's buddies. "Don't be foolish," he said, just loud enough to be heard over the noise of the music. "Get your buddy out of the sun and behave." The even tone of authority and menace was enough to stop whatever plans were lurking at the back of their brains. They stood and sneered. Gruen moved off, sliding through the crowd, his eyes moving lightly over men in the crowd, searching.

"Well I'll be damned," said Meade as he wheeled into a parking slot among the thousand vehicles that spread out over the desert in an irregular mass of hot, shining metal and glass. "Look at that." He pointed ahead of the wagon. There was the van with SANTINI PIZZA painted on the rear doors.

"Looks like everyone's here, Meade," Hannah sighed. "Regular old home week. Do you think Gruen was sent a special invitation?"

Meade leaned back in the seat, checking the rearview mirror; no one seemed too interested in the car.

"Look, there must be a couple of thousand people down there. I want to find out what the hell makes me so interesting." He smiled at Hannah, but she looked out the window. "Hey, it's safer here than out on the road, you know? No one expects me, exactly."

"It's like the dog, Meade. I wish you hadn't left Mike with the car salesman."

"We couldn't take him with us. We've got a border crossing that's not going to be any fun. The dog would have given us away sooner or later. And the guy was an animal lover."

"But someone could find the dog."

"Who knows about the husky? There's been nothing in the papers or on television. The Brigadier would have covered up at the farm."

Hannah shifted in the seat. "Or the FBI is keeping the whole thing out of the press."

"Could be, but I don't think so."

"Gruen knew about the dogs."

"Gruen isn't going to find us. He's pretty good, but we could have gone any way out of Missoula. He's not psychic. He'll play his best hunch, I think, and that's

Canada. Hell, maybe we should have done it through Canada."

"I think the whole thing is nuts, Meade. Why did you take the dog from the farm in the first place? Why did you drop him off so obviously. It's like . . . Well, it's strange. Almost like you want to leave a trail or something."

Meade took her hand. "You're catching on. I'm laying a light trail. It's got to be done very carefully. Nothing too obvious. If Gruen is already up in Canada, so much the better. The FBI isn't going to let him run around loose. They know he's pretty good and they'll be keeping an eye on him. If he draws a lot of heat up north, that makes it easier for us to get into Mexico. And if he's headed south, he's going to pick up that little hint, maybe."

"But why the hell do you want him to do that? It seems stupid." Hannah squeezed his hand hard. Meade pulled her over against him.

"Because if that happens and I can spot the action that Gruen will draw, we simply beat it back north or over to Florida, or anywhere, while he's hanging around here, thinking he's found the end of the rainbow."

Hannah pulled back from him, with a smile. "That's all so complicated. It's a game, isn't it? It's like chess for you?"

Meade laughed. "Come on, let's go hear the music and drink some beer and say good-bye to J. R. Meade. He's going to be gone a long time, I hope. He deserves a last drink and a good send-off." Meade opened the door and pulled Hannah out with him into the baking heat and clear air of the desert. They sauntered hand in hand toward the loud sounds of the music, oddly mournful in the brilliant sunshine.

New Mexico, RNK-177. That was the number Gruen searched for on every Chevrolet coupe among the growing number of cars that spread over the desert. He walked slowly through the rows, trying to look as though he were just a middle-aged tourist attracted by all the excitement. From the vantage of the hill behind the crowd earlier, Gruen had gained little information, except to marvel at the number of people, swollen to at least three thousand, and at the lack of portable toilets. There was only one usable road out of Oracle, Route 77, which ran either back toward Tucson or Northeast toward New Mexico. If Meade were around, he'd have to use it.

Gruen examined every car he found of the right description and there were several. All had New Mexico plates, but not RNK-177. Some had the evidence of family use, with stuffed toys, picnic hampers, and the like, although Gruen didn't put such a trick past Meade. The cars were spread out over a wide area and he could find no vantage point to watch them all.

Naturally Meade would have changed plates. It would be stupid not to. But then leaving the dog and the Brigadier's Jeep was stupid. Gruen leaned against the hood of a car in the heat and considered. Meade was too good to be so obvious. Unless he wanted to be found. Why would he want that? To confront him and kill him? Gruen couldn't believe that Meade thought him such an adversary when the whole country was looking for him. And what were the chances that Gruen would come down that highway and spot the dog? Not great. Maybe Meade knew what he was doing. And maybe Gruen was being sucked into a "light" trail, an old Special Forces trick.

Gruen continued to saunter through the parked cars,

his feet beginning to hurt. He passed a van that said
SANTINI PIZZA, DETROIT, MICHIGAN. Crazy, he thought, what
brought people together. Behind him the noise of the
music seemed far away under the great noise of the crowd.
It sounded like a football game every time a new musician
was introduced. There was only one thing to do now, and
that was to wade through that mass of humanity and look
at every face. If any of the FBI agents recognized him, he
was in for some sharp questioning about his presence. He
smiled. He'd have to be as careful as J. R. Meade. He
headed down the rise toward the sound of revelry.

Westfield Monroe stood in the shade of the emergency
medical tent that the Tucson Red Cross had erected.
There were prostrate forms on several cots being min-
istered to by volunteers in white jackets. He scribbled in
his notebook, getting the old man's story right.

What a tale! About the Walk Softly coat, the man and
woman in the desert who tested it with him and left him
$500. Christ, he thought, it's like Pretty Boy Floyd or
Robin Hood. That man had to be J. R. Meade. One of
the heat prostration victims moaned. Westfield was struck
by the thought that the old man was probably one of the
few people that had seen Meade face to face since the
skyjacking. Santini would recognize him! He ran out of
the tent, his eyes searching the crowd for the old geezer
in the padded coat.

"You're him, ain't you?" whispered Elijah Santini as
he sat down beside the young couple who looked as if
they'd just come down from a mountain backpacking

expedition. Among the thousands of people sitting on the desert floor, taking in the music, while here and there a knot of people danced and swayed standing up, Meade and Hannah looked ordinary enough, but Elijah had spotted them after only a few minutes.

"You going to start that, Elijah?" Meade smiled, but his eyes were roving the crowd. Hannah held Meade's hand in a panicked grip.

"Him." Elijah nodded toward the great cloth banner stretched over the bandstand where a lone woman in a frilly dress sang a song about cheating love. On the banner was the drawing of Meade in his green beret.

"Elijah, it doesn't matter who that guy is, or who I am, does it? We're friends. Now, that's enough."

Elijah looked around. "Thanks for the money and all. You want to be careful, pard. Cops, FBI. A reporter from *Time* magazine. They're all over the place."

"I'll be careful. How's the coat going?"

"Tried to talk to the feds and the cops here. They think I'm a fart in a windstorm."

"How'd you like to sell your van, Elijah? I can give you a better price than the dealers."

Elijah wouldn't look at Meade but talked out of the side of his mouth like a character in a spy movie. "Why would you do that?"

"I'll give you twenty thousand for it, and my wagon."

"*Twenty* thousand?"

"Hush," Meade hissed. "Twenty grand. But you have to do one little service for me."

Elijah smiled and warmed to the conspiracy. "Anything, pard, anything."

Westfield saw the old man sneaking out of the crowd, looking around like he was carrying a load of dynamite.

Behind him Westfield was struck by the couple in back-packing shorts who were making their way to the edge of the crowd on the opposite side. He worked his way quickly through the massed bodies, mumbling "excuse mes" and, at a dead run, came up behind the man and woman. "Hey, wait up!" he called quietly. J. R. Meade, hardly recognizable under his rimless glasses and mustache, turned around and calmly looked at the *Time* reporter.

"This is getting to be a regular receiving line," Meade said to the young man.

Monroe was nearly speechless. The handsome woman with Meade must be his wife. She looked apprehensive, ready to run, but Meade looked cool enough. "I'm, ah, Westfield Monroe from *Time* magazine. I wondered if you had a few minutes to answer some questions?"

Meade laughed; an open, honest one, Westfield noted. "I'm just a little busy right now, fella, if you want to talk, come along, but keep it quiet and natural. Also, you might get shot at. You guys get combat pay?"

"Look, there's cops all over here, I . . . ."

"Are you crazy, Meade," Hannah hissed, as she looked wildly around.

"Not exactly. Mr. *Time* magazine is going to make us a threesome. Nobody's looking for a threesome, are they?" Meade shifted his gaze to Westfield. "And I don't think he wants his story blown either." Meade took Hannah's hand. They walked briskly toward the parking lot, West-field Monroe trotting to keep up.

Gruen felt the electric jolt of recognition. No matter what people did to disguise themselves, it was the backs of their necks that always gave them away. When he saw

the slim, tall man from the rear, walking up the rise toward the maze of parked cars, he knew it was Meade.

Hannah was with him. Gruen recognized something
besides the back of her head, too, he smiled. All he had
to do was walk up to the FBI agent who stood with his
finger pressed to earpiece, listening to reports of God
knew what, and it would be over. Or just show his badge
to the cops by the patrol car a hundred yards up the rise.
He had J. R. Meade as surely as he ever would. The
empty raft floated through his mind as he walked briskly
up the hill, twenty-five yards behind Meade and Hannah
and another man.

Gruen had won. Meade was his for the taking. He
thought of the money, stashed somewhere, but dismissed
it. It didn't matter. What mattered was that he'd gambled
and won.

As he followed, Gruen was struck by a thunderclap of
understanding: He hadn't won. If Meade thought Gruen
was going to show up, how could he know that he
wouldn't report him to the assembled lawmen, that he
wouldn't alert them? Meade knew his adversary. Gruen
was not going to turn over a general alarm and have the
massed cops and agents galloping after his prize. He was
going to track him to someplace private, someplace
where he could take him alone, and that might get
tricky. He almost burst out laughing. Meade wasn't
lucky, he was goddamn smart. It was a draw.

Just as Gruen reached the top of the rise over which
Meade and Hannah had disappeared a moment before,
someone behind him screamed, "I saw him! There he is!
It's J. R. Meade! It's *him*!" The cops to Gruen's left and
an FBI agent were already running toward the sound.
The chant was picked up through the crowd, "It's *him*!
It's *him*!" The cops were wading in toward the noise,
their sticks raised, and the FBI agents had drawn their

service revolvers and were scampering around the edge
of the vast bowl of humanity.

The music stopped, The Lonesome Cowboys peered
into the crowd, holding their instruments and pointing
in different directions. The beer and sun had taken its
toll on sanity, and fights broke out through the crowd.
Hostility toward the police was a living animal. A young
patrolman shoved a girl, a man shoved back. The club
came down on his wrist, someone grabbed the policeman
from behind, and he disappeared under a pile of half-
naked bodies.

The noise level rose and Gruen's eyes swept the parking lot. He saw a figure dive into a car. An old Chevy!
Meade was getting out. Gruen was trotting through the
line of cars when an FBI agent popped out from behind
a trunk and leveled a revolver at his chest. "Hold it right
there. I am a federal agent. Don't move."

"You asshole," Gruen said evenly, "get out of my
way. I'm a federal agent, too." Gruen showed the man
his FAA identity card and left him open mouthed,
holding his pistol in a dangling arm as he sprinted to his
car.

He weaved through the parking lot as those sane
enough to realize that an impending riot was due in the
crowd below ran for their cars. Several vehicles, including
a police car with sirens full blast, made it onto the highway before Gruen.

The car had been headed toward Tucson, that much
Gruen had seen before dust and other cars had cut off
his view. Gruen streaked along the road, the hot rubber
singing on the melting asphalt. Had the police spotted
Meade? Or the Bureau? Had they recognized him, for
that matter? The FBI agent who'd stopped him was
hopefully too busy to put together his name and ID—
by now a marked one in the Bureau—and his presence in

Oracle. Several cars came into view as he rounded a wide
curve through some piles of rock that were sprinkled
across the desert. None of them was a dark Chevrolet.
Then Gruen noticed tire tracks that left the curve of the
highway and led away into the desert toward a hump of
loose boulders a half-mile distant. He pulled off the road
and backed up to the tracks. No police cars were in sight.
The tracks were fresh and not too deep. The vehicle
which made them was traveling at some speed. But there
was no dust cloud. The time scheme fit, figuring the lead
that Meade had on him.

He drove slowly toward the pile of rocks. Meade would
be watching his approach. If he ran, Gruen would spot
him easily and could chase him with the advantage of
having the law all around. It was not the way Gruen
wanted it to end, but maybe it would have to be. Gruen
was not afraid. Meade wouldn't shoot.

He might try for the tire, though, or the engine, if he
had the right armament. The thing to do would be to
stop here, a good four hundred yards out, and radio for
help. Gruen braked the government Plymouth and
looked at the radio. He didn't even have it turned on
and tuned to the police band that would be handling the
festival. The slow grind of bureaucracy wouldn't run
down a loner, a man trained to function in a vacuum.
The hot wind of the desert sifted through the car. To
hell with it. Meade was waiting, he felt sure. Full of
surprises.

He drove quietly and slowly into the shadow of the
great jumbled rise of stone, the air cooler there. There
was no sign of life. The tire tracks arched around the
stone, some seventy-five feet in diameter, out of sight.

Gruen took the .38 from his holster, checked the
cylinder, and got out. The silence overwhelmed him.
He stood for a moment in the wind, letting it blow some

of the tension from him. If Meade were going to shoot, it would have to be now. No sense worrying about it.

The sound of singing drifted to Gruen on the wind. It sounded like a hymn. He smiled to himself. Meade was getting gaga in his old age.

He walked carefully around the outcroppings of boulders and spotted the rear end of the station wagon. The singing was louder, a thin voice crooning, "I walk in the garden alone, while the dew is still on the roses, and the voice I hear, falling on my ear, the Son of God, discloses, Oh, I walk with him and I talk with him, and he tells me I am his own . . ."

Gruen ran stooped over to the rear of the Chevy. Peering through the back window he saw an old man, dressed in a coat that looked like an ironing-board cover, sitting on the hood, staring out at the desert and singing. The singing stopped. "Somebody there?" He peered around.

Gruen stood up, his gun ready, and walked up in front of the fellow. But it was some crazy old codger.

"Well, well, Johnny Lawman. How you today?"

"I'm just fine, old timer." Gruen was amused. "What's the story?"

"The story is a long one, my friend. It involves fear and deception and the delivery of pizza and a coat called Walk Softly."

"Pizza?" Gruen felt the glimmer of something. The oldest trick in the book. "Are you from Detroit?"

"That I am. *Was* from Detroit is more accurate, though." He looked content.

Santini Pizza, Detroit, Michigan. Gruen had a vision of a red van. Meade had switched horses on him. "Hey Johnny Law, you'll never get him," the old man cackled.

Gruen left the old man on the car hood and trotted back to his car. He was at the wheel, the motor turning over, and he grabbed the microphone on the radio. He pushed down the talk button. But he didn't say a word. Meade. He wanted him. An APB now would do it, certainly. But Gruen wanted him alone and sure and swift. The chase meant too much to him now to broadcast the alarm. He slammed the microphone back in its clip and wheeled back toward the road, tires spewing dust and gravel.

Meade sat on the cushioned bench in the chartreuse and stainless steel of the van. Elijah had started that little ruckus down the hill after moving Meade's gear into the van, and then beat it in the Chevy. It wasn't very sophisticated, but not bad for thinking on your feet. If the FBI or Gruen or anyone was onto the car, this little trick would buy him some time.

The curtains just behind the driver's section of the van were pulled tight, except for a tiny crack, where Hannah crouched and peeked out through the windshield. The boy from *Time* was scribbling madly in his notebook, had been asking rapid-fire questions for almost fifteen minutes, while they could hear the police sirens, and the yells of protesters being thrown into the paddy wagons that had arrived from Tucson. The band had started to play again. There was still a sizable crowd down the hill; for The Lonesome Cowboys were cutting a live album, and the mini-riot only added to it.

Westfield Monroe had exhausted his supply of questions. Now, he could only think of his exclusive interview, his photo featured on the Publisher's Memo page, maybe a raise. There was only one big zinger left, and he wasn't sure how to deliver it. He'd been impressed with Meade, a calm strong individual who hated bureaucracy, being told what to do, and maybe still sore over what the army had done to him in Vietnam, and with a fine sense of humor. But none of it seemed to explain the man. There was an elusive quality to Meade, something that couldn't be pinned down, one that lurked in the shadows of his words and actions. But Westfield had to ask.

"You've been very kind, Mr. Meade, and I've just got one final question."

"That's good because it's just about time to get out of here." Meade smiled, apparently in no hurry.

"Why did you do it?"

"What?" Meade leaned forward, the smile gone from his face. Hannah turned from her vantage point at the curtains and looked at Meade.

"Why did you skyjack the plane?"

The question hung in the chartreuse interior of the van. In one corner Westfield could see a pair of bright-blue backpacks. He was looking at nearly three-quarters of a million dollars, he thought.

"It was an exercise." Meade looked thoughtful, as if there was a further answer that he couldn't vocalize, that he didn't know.

"Exercise?" Westfield was puzzled and asked as he scribbled down the words.

"I don't know exactly. But we've all been learning from it, haven't we?"

"Meade," Hannah pleaded, "let's get out of here. You're starting to get dumb. You're going to get caught. And what are we going to do about him?" She inclined her head toward Westfield. A wave of fear came over Westfield. After all this guy had skyjacked a plane. He was armed—a shotgun stood propped weirdly against the chartreuse-carpeted wall. Bonnie and Clyde. Westfield felt weak.

Meade smiled. "Well, he's going to get out of the van

and go call his office and tell them he's got an exclusive story, and he won't stop off to tell the cops because he'd blow it. Right?" He smiled evenly at Westfield.

"That's right. I mean, if I blew the whistle, it wouldn't do me any good." Westfield thought that's just what he'd do. He wiped sweat from his forehead.

Hannah shook her head. She slid through the curtains and started the van. Meade opened the door for the reporter. After Westfield stepped down, Meade stayed in the shadow of the van door and said, "Hey, kid. I shouldn't bullshit you any longer. My wife thought it would be a lark to put you on. My name's Elijah Santini from Detroit, I've got a pizza business there. My dad's a bit cracked, see, and he's running around telling people I'm J. R. Meade. Hell, I'm not Meade. Can you imagine Meade showing up here? He'd have to be stupid. I just look a little like the guy.

"I didn't want you to ruin your career reporting the story. Sometimes the old lady goes too far. You stop and see me when you're in Detroit and the pizza's on me. Okay?" He shut the door and the van moved off at a peaceable speed, weaving through the parking lot and past the police vehicles parked at the driveway.

Westfield Monroe looked up at the sky, an empty blue bowl of hot air. "Goddamn it," he swore, and threw his notebook on the ground. Then he started to laugh. A cop began walking toward him, thinking no doubt that another unruly drunk had been out in the sun too long.

In Superior, Arizona, northeast of Tucson, Meade pulled the van into a slot by a low, concrete-rock building that housed the Helpee-Selfee Laundromat. They left the keys in the van, took their packs, and drove off in a 1963 yellow Dodge convertible with ripped, red leatherette upholstery, in which the keys had been left. Not a soul saw them arrive or leave the quiet town at noon, four days before Christmas.

At a phone booth outside of Oracle, Westfield Monroe talked to New York. He was sweating, squinting his eyes against the desert glare. A string of tinsel Christmas ornaments hung between the gas pumps and the station where his car was being serviced. Westfield felt ten feet tall. He was Joseph Pulitzer, Woodward, Bernstein, and Breslin rolled into one. "Elinor, I've got an exclusive interview with J. R. Meade. Do you want me to Telex it or give it to a girl over the phone now?"

"Westfield? Are you still in Arizona? Christ, you're just what we need. Another J. R. Meade exclusive."

"What do you mean?"

"Our Seattle bureau chief paid a thousand dollars for an exclusive interview with J. R. Meade. A right-winger magazine in Bakersfield, California, tried to sell us an exclusive interview with him, full of James Earl Ray stuff. Reuters says J. R. Meade has been spotted in Havana as Castro's guest. J. R. Meade exclusives are big business this week. And besides, we've had to kill the feature. They decided upstairs that the Petro-War is this week's story."

"But this really *was* J. R. Meade, goddamnit, Elinor."

"Sure it was. Now come home and go hang around Bloomingdale's."

After he hung up, Westfield stood for a moment in the hot phone booth. Maybe Meade was right. Take the money and run, run to your dream. Because the bastards will never give you an inch. Not one column inch. And now it was back to Bloomies to see what was new in goose-down vests. Lifestyles. That wasn't the right name for it, somehow, Westfield thought as he shambled back to his car, waiting like a false promise in the hot sunshine.

8

THE CLIFF

Cowlic, GuVo, Vaya Chin, Silver Bell. The names were as strange as the place. In the shadow of the Santa Rosa Mountain range, Gruen drove on the slim band of blacktop through the Papago Indian Reservation. The Indians here were lost to ancient grace; stiff, strange forms that came out of the mountain mists in woolen coats, sheep milling about them. A peaceful, blasted, hopeless people, distrusting the reservation agents, government doctors, federal veterinarians, Peace Corps ditch-diggers, and marshals that punished the drunks and confiscated their firearms. In his gray, interagency motor-pool Plymouth Gruen was just another slab of white man's law, moving through sacred ground. Gruen's friend Willie, strong man of the docks, over a game of nine-ball in a Tacoma pool hall one night, said, "If there were two guys left on earth, Bill, one would ask the other for a government job."

A fat child in a thin shirt ran across the road ten yards

ahead of the Plymouth. White fog streamed from his nostrils, his black hair flying, and as he paused to enter through the blanket across the doorway of a log and mud Hogan, he fastened his black, bottomless eyes on Gruen. Gruen had seen the same looks in the eyes of white men in Seattle and natives in Vietnam, the look that said you were the authority, expect no quarter; you would be given none.

Gruen drove relentlessly toward nothing. It was the last hunch he had to play. In a way it was funny. Meade was very good, suckering him with the old switched-car routine. The trail was cold now, and nothing could resurrect it. Studying the maps of Arizona and Mexico the night before Gruen thought like a soldier, the way Meade would have to think now; now that the heat was on.

If Meade were headed for the Mexican border, which way would he go? There were a thousand miles of that dotted line on the map. If it were Gruen's to do, he'd hole up for a few days, hide out, and plan. There'd have to be careful preparations. A location would have to be scouted, maybe disguises arranged, and some way to make that big bundle of cash look inconspicuous. The FBI had redoubled its border efforts. The Texas Rangers, United States Customs, and the border patrol were all in on it now. They were combing the border towns of Nogales, Lukeville, and Douglas all the way to El Paso in the east.

But Gruen believed that Meade would stay away from towns, from civilization. His whole run from Missoula to Arizona had been through the edges of settled America. He got no nearer than he had to. If the J.R. Meade Festival had been held in the Phoenix Memorial Arena, Meade would never have shown. It was still an odd fact of life in America that the woods and the wilderness were the best places to go unseen. Most criminals made the mistake of trying to hide in a city like New York or L.A., and the odds were simply not with them. That was the movies' idea.

And on the map the place that looked best and closest—for Meade would want to get to ground quickly —was the Papago Reservation. It had the advantage of being on the Mexican border in a wild, unpopulated area. And it was there that Gruen had started to look. There was little hope. All he could do was try to outguess his old pupil. But the pupil knew the instructor was on the trail. What would that do to the game?

Ahead Gruen spotted a store, a general goods affair, a private one, leased out by the government to some white man, to sell groceries and wine and supplies to the Indians. Gruen pulled in before the clapboard building, which seemed to be totally out of plumb, leaning in some corners as if it would fall over.

On the narrow, raised porch an old Indian man stood, looking out at the endless vista of scrub. He took no notice of Gruen. Gruen bought cheese, bread, and a six-pack of Diet Pepsi, an odd drink for an Indian reservation store, he thought. He sat in the car breaking off chunks of the Monterey Jack and folding bread around it, sipping the cola.

Gruen glanced at the few other vehicles parked in front of the store. There was a pickup with all four fenders missing, an ancient Ford tractor, and a yellow convertible. Indians, thought Gruen, had the oddest vehicles that he'd ever seen, including that rattletrap panel truck that the Brigadier's Indian in Montana was so fond of. As he ate, Gruen read the bumper sticker that had been plastered at a cockeyed angle on the yellow convertible's door. "Impeach Earl Warren." What the hell did Indians know about Earl Warren? And Indians didn't give a good goddamn about impeach, either. Something didn't sit right with Gruen. Why hadn't the Indian, who no doubt bought the car from a white used-car dealer somewhere, torn off the sign? Was it pure laziness? Also the top was down and the morning cold would make it too chilly to drive that way. Didn't the top work?

Gruen lay the cheese and bread on the seat beside him, and taking the Diet Pepsi, sauntered over to the car. He laid his hand on the hood. Cold. It hadn't been run recently. He walked along the side of the car, looking into its interior. It was clean except for a pair of battery jumper cables in the rear floor and an old tow rope.

Gruen looked at the tow rope and began to smile. Then he laughed, long and loud, and smacked the fender of the convertible. The old Indian on the porch didn't even glance his way. Crazy white man, probably drunk. Gruen looked again at the thick, greasy length of hemp on the back floor. In one end of it, perfectly tied as if for mounting on an instruction board, was a double carrick hitch, a sailor's knot he'd read about in the book at Hannah's house. A knot to tie two big lines together. It was a complicated one that resembled several interlocking pretzels. Gruen walked briskly up the stairs of the store, past the Indian and into the place, where the owner, an elderly frail man balanced on a chair, was tying a tinsel message across the ceiling. "Merry Christmas," it said.

"How did you know about this place?" Hannah's words reverberated off the adobe and stone in the cold shadows. The wind whistled by the opening in the face of the mesa, two hundred feet above the ground. Meade was pulling the long, government-supplied rope ladder up the face of the cliff toward him, piling it neatly in folds by the twin iron bolts driven into the stone floor to hold it. When he finished, he came over to her breathing quickly from the exertion.

"It's called *Casa Negro*. It's one of the oldest cliff dwellings in America, but it isn't famous because it's in such disrepair and the archaeologists want it left alone. They're afraid to restore it because it might all fall down." When she had first seen it, a mile off, after they'd backpacked the six miles from the little store on the reservation out through the wilds of the place, Hannah thought the mesa, rising like a cube of red rock, with its face split open by the towering cave, resembled a huge eye, looking impassively out for enemies.

"That means "black house'? *Casa Negro*?"

"Probably because it's deeper than most of these cliff dwellings, and always full of shadows." Meade picked up the backpack with the money in it, which was still wrapped like supermarket beer in Saran Wrap, twenty-seven packages of it. The backpack also held the broken-down shotgun and the .45 automatic pistol, borrowed from the Brigadier's collection.

"In Nam there was a Papago Indian who told me about this place. It's old. These adobe bricks were made a thousand years before Christ and by 1,000 A.D. it was abandoned. No one knows why. The Indian told me that he played here as a kid, that it was a marvelous place, and that the government had put in the rope ladder, but no one ever came except a few scientists. We were close by and needed a place to figure out how we'll cross the border. So here we are at lovely and exciting *Casa Negro*."

"Maybe that Indian who told you about it will show up here."

Meade was gently pulling an aged, adobe brick from a wall which curved around some ceremonial room, making a hole in the wall. "He was caught by the VC. I found his head on a stick, Hannah."

"Stop it, Meade. Goddamn you and your war." She stalked off to sit on a crumbling piece of a house nearby, staring out at the brilliant desert which, seen through the black-shadowed opening of the cave, looked like a huge movie set. Nothing stirred.

Meade said nothing. He took the stacks of money in their plastic wrappers and fitted them tightly into the opening he'd made, and when he was finished, he put the .45 on top of the pile. He carefully fit the two adobe blocks back over the opening, threw the three blocks from the center layer of the wall into a corner of the adjoining room, and scuffed up the pile of adobe dust he'd made on the floor of the dwelling. He came over to Hannah.

"Look, the Brigadier used to tell me when I got back from Nam, that if you fought in one, you believed that your war was the most important one in history. Vietnam was a silly little piece of shit. I saw people I liked get killed for a patch of nothing. I'm sorry, Hannah. I didn't mean to be gory."

He walked to the edge of the cliff. "I wanted this whole thing to be bloodless, or it was no good. That evil bastard Remson is dead and the old man is injured. I want to stop thinking about death."

"Then why did you do all this?" Hannah followed him to the cliff edge. "You saw Gruen back at that concert just like I did. Why didn't you leave? Why did we go in the first place? It's as if you're teasing Gruen, taunting everyone. It's hide-and-go-seek for you, Meade. Damn, it's childish. You're going to get caught.

"You say you just want to get out and go sailing. You say society is shit. I agree, it is. But why take so many chances? We could have been across the border by now." She sighed and straightened her back, as if saying what was on her mind had relieved some ache.

Meade stared out at the desert. "Because the game is

the reason. Maybe that sounds stupid, but the only time I have the feeling of living is when I'm getting away from them. I want to sail around the world, and I've always wanted that. But this part isn't bad, Hannah. It's like figuring out a navigational chart. Where are you going, and can it be plotted? If I think I'm going to go live on Tahiti like a native and eat pineapples forever, I'll go crazy. I can't stop being restless, Hannah. I've tried, and then I want to go out and play with the big boys."

"I don't know what got into us, Meade. You're a crazy bastard. But I love you. You *are* one of the big boys. I want to play with you, too." She looked around her at the fascinating shapes of the cliff dwelling. "Let's go exploring."

"All right," Meade said. He assembled the shotgun, and they set off. The cliff dwelling extended two hundred and fifty feet from side to side. It was, near the center, eighty feet deep, narrowing into the core of the mesa. There were three large, circular areas, ritual centers for the men of the tribe, and some fifty small, one-room dwellings in various states of age. Much of the dwelling was merely piles of adobe pieces, shards of building that were returning to desert dust. Several places near the rear of the dwelling, archaeologists had roped off small excavations, where overturned rocks were shellacked and numbered.

It was an afternoon of silence, high above the desert; they were safe for a while against all the pursuit the world could bring on them. Later in the evening, they made love slowly on top of the sleeping bags, the desert spread out below them in the moonlight like a well-lit mystery. Before she fell asleep that night in the down sleeping bag Hannah took Meade's hand and said, "I don't know about you, but if this is being out of the action, I could do with a whole lot more of it."

"Me too," Meade smiled. After she was asleep, which was very quickly after the exertions of the day and evening, Meade sat with a penlight and studied the map of Mexico. It was three days before Christmas. That was a big holiday in Mexico. And in a border town like Nogales, thousands of celebrants passed back and forth across the border. He'd planned a crossing in the wilds of the Sonora-Baja area, but they would surely have greater border patrols now. Road travel in Mexico would be light. If he guessed right, the chances were better in Nogales, right under the assembled but confused noses of the authorities, and more fun, too. It was going to have to be very good.

He thought for a long while and then Meade flicked the penlight over the United States topographical map, looking for the little cross symbols for churches. He found one that he thought would work, put the map down, and fell into a dreamless sleep.

His foot found nothing but air, and Gruen's mind shrieked "No!" in the darkness; he wobbled, his cold fingers losing a grip on the smooth stone of the old steps carved in the mesa. Finally his booted foot struck into a step-hole and he steadied himself with a sickening attempt at equilibrium. His hands had grasped the ancient stone so tightly that he could feel the warm blood from his savaged palms against the coldness of skin on his wrists. Wind howled in long gusts of power in the desert night, and Gruen clung to the edge of the *Casa Negro* mesa wondering if he'd finally gone too far to get back again. Gruen couldn't know it, but he was almost two hundred feet above the level of the huge boulders and sharp shards of rock that skirted the mesa. That fact would not have made him happier.

He clung desperately, holding the small flashlight in his teeth, kept awake and on the edge of sanity by the pain of his hands. He began to climb again, feeling his way almost blindly from handhold to handhold. Gruen had learned about the hand-hewn stairway up the back of the mesa, on the opposite side from the opening of the cliff-dwelling site, from the owner of the store on the reservation. The man's loquacious nature—confiding to another white man—had been revved up by the application of two fifty-dollar bills to his palm.

No one had seen who'd left the yellow convertible, maybe it had been stolen by one of the damn warhoops and abandoned out there, the store owner thought. And if, as Gruen had asked, a young Indian on the run— solid wink there—wanted to hide out nearby, where might he go? *Casa Negro* was explained to Gruen in great detail, and the funny story about how a young buck every now and then gets shitfaced and goes up there and pulls up the ladder, and how the damn reservation police then have to climb up the back of the mesa in the hand-holds of an old escape route, and how they even left a coil of rope up on top to rappel down into the dwelling to get the hungover braves out of the place. That's surely where a young Indian in trouble with the feds would go hide, all right.

And that, thought Gruen, is why I'm out here swinging around in the wind. Maybe the old bastard was on the side of the Indians and was trying to get me to kill myself. But Gruen doubted it. Before he'd begun climbing the tract of little step-holes up the mesa, he'd driven back around near the front of the cliff dwelling. Sure enough the ladder was pulled up. He tried to stay out of sight and hustled once more around the back of the huge rock and began climbing, armed only with his .38 pistol, a flashlight, a coil of rope bought at the general store in case the owner had been wrong about the reservation police foresight.

It was nearly 4:00 A.M. when Gruen reached the end of the step-holes and could feel ahead that the angle of ascent had dropped considerably. He'd have to wait until dawn before he tried to rappel down the face of the cliff into the opening. And Meade would surely be waiting. The question was, Gruen thought, as he settled down to wait for first light, would Meade be awake for it, or would Gruen have a chance?

He wasn't quite as afraid of being shot off the rope as he was of dangling there, swinging back and forth, while Meade laughed at him. That would be worse than shooting. Gruen prayed to the gods of the darkness that no shooting would take place. And then he dozed.

When Meade woke, he became totally awake, as he had in Vietnam, with alarm and with nerves tingling. It wasn't right. It had gone very bad. His hands hit the stone floor, he flipped into a sitting position, his right hand reaching out for the shotgun. It was missing. Gruen.

Gruen sat on a low, crumbling wall five yards away. The shotgun across his lap. His face was smeared with dirt as well as his clothes. His hands were raw with patches of skin missing. He was obviously in pain, but the blue eyes under the short gray hair and jutting brows were cool and amused. "Good morning, Meade," he said quietly. Hannah still slept, bundled against the morning chill, her head buried in the sleeping bag.

"Shit." Meade was still coming out of sleep, though his body was alert. He thought fleetingly of a sailboat on the great, blue Pacific. It was sliding under the waves. "How the hell did you get here? You must have flown."

Gruen shifted the double-barreled gun until it was pointing directly between Meade and Hannah. Behind him the great ball of the sun was emerging from the horizon, sending shimmering waves of light through the organ pipe cactus, sagebrush, and rocks. To one side of the opening of the cliff dwelling Meade saw a rope dangling down from above, swaying gently in the morning breeze.

"I didn't fly," Gruen said, blotting his bleeding hand on his trouser leg. "But I'll let you in on a secret. The Indians who built this place were not the smartest redmen in the desert. There's a whole set of steps up the back of the mesa. Getting down into here is a little hard, though. And climbing in the dark's no fun either."

Gruen was obviously enjoying himself, Meade thought. He didn't blame him. He'd done the near-impossible, and alone. In fact Meade kind of admired his old sergeant, smiling like he'd just swallowed the biggest canary in the world.

Hannah awoke, twisting and stretching in her sleeping bag. When she opened her eyes to see Gruen and the gun, she said only, "Oh, my God."

"I don't know how you feel, but I could use some coffee," Gruen smiled. "Should we go into town for it, or do you have some here?"

"In the pack there's a burner and a packet of instant," Hannah told him. She climbed slowly out of her bag, dressed in Levis, shirt, and socks. She pulled on her boots, and both men watched her in silence, as if there was nothing more to say.

As she went for the blue pack by the back wall, Gruen said quietly, "Do everything slowly, Hannah. I wouldn't want you to try to get a weapon out of that bag."

"I didn't know you two were on a first-name basis," Meade said, calculating exactly what tack this confrontation was going to take, cataloging alternatives.

"I had dinner with your wife in Missoula, Meade, when you were still among the missing. That's all."

"I guess she loves me because I'm such a great escape artist," Meade said. "Mind if I get up and stretch?"

"Just don't be stupid. Don't come out of there with a handgun or anything. I don't want this to be bloody. And I can't think how I'd get you down if you were wounded." Hannah returned with a small primus stove and set it burning, putting a canteen of water over the small ring of blue flame to heat. For a moment they all watched it in silence.

"How the hell did you find me?" Meade shook his head, as he climbed slowly out of his sleeping bag. It was a professional question, cut off from the situation. And Gruen's answer was the same.

"A monkey's fist, a sheepshank, and a carrick hitch."

Meade laughed. A strange and joyful sound echoing through the great hall of the cliff dwellings. "Well, I'll be damned. I *knew* you were marking me, I knew you were on to something. You came too close in Missoula and at that festival. Hey, Sarge, can you imagine a festival for me?" There was an uneasy camaraderie between the two men. Hannah shook her head.

"I'm surprised they didn't sing 'For He's a Jolly Good Fellow,' Meade," said Gruen smiling. "And you really threw me a sucker punch in that parking lot. Damn, I was sure I had you. It's like the old VC tunnel entrances; you thought you had them all covered and the bastards would pop out from under a hootch two villages over."

"You two have a real admiration society going here, don't you?" Hannah was pouring hot water from the canteen into two metal Sierra cups. "But what the hell happens now, Gruen. Do you turn us in?"

"I've thought about that a lot." Gruen looked weary. There were bags under his eyes, and his hands looked like raw meat. He sat slumped but alert. "I thought about it out there with a flashlight in my teeth, climbing in those damn little steps up a thousand feet to the top of the mesa in the dark, and I thought about it all the way down that rope into the cave here, while I could smell my hands burn. I wondered, what the hell I was killing myself for? What was it all going to come to? One more alleged felon in jail and the money back in the vault."

"And you decided to be a nice guy, huh, Sarge? You're going to let us go? Where are the troops? You must have called in a dawn raid. Hell, I expect mortars and artillery." Meade was tired of the game, the way it was going. Now he'd play it bitter and see what he could stir up. Gruen sat with the gun still pointed carelessly between him and Hannah as they sat sipping coffee. Hannah finished hers and stood up from the pile of rocks where she'd sat with the sleeping bag wrapped around her legs. She poured more hot water and instant coffee in the cup and passed it to Gruen. Gruen stared at the coffee.

"No one knows I'm here, Meade. This was a little exercise between you and me. I've read a lot of guff in the papers about how you hate society and just want to get out of it and take some bankroll with you. But that's bullshit. You just wanted a real good chase, you bastard." Gruen looked up; he was smiling. He reached for the coffee cup and winced in pain. "I can't hold the damn cup. And I need that coffee, Hannah. Would you come over here and hold it for me?"

Hannah did as she was asked. "Get on the other side, away from Meade please," Gruen said. "So you won't be in the way."

"Sarge, I think you needed a good chase, too. And you're still pretty good at it. Why aren't you still in the army?"

"They wanted me to train troops and recruit."

"But who's going to teach the kids how to be as good as you?" Meade watched Gruen's bloody hands, but there was no advantage he could spot.

"The kids don't need to be as good as you or me, Meade. What the hell for? So they can skyjack airliners?"

"So they can survive," Meade said.

"Let's get this over with," Hannah snapped. "It's finished. Let's go. You two can have old home week for Green Berets after we're locked up in jail." She walked to the edge of the cliff and pushed over the neat folds of the rope ladder, which went clacking and banging down from the face of the cliff.

"How did you know we were up here?" Meade asked quietly. Gruen had half-turned to watch Hannah, and Meade wanted to keep his head moving, his mind busy with details. Because Hannah was wrong. It wasn't over quite yet. Gruen's attention snapped back to Meade. "After I found the car at the store, I talked to the owner."

"Did you drive out here?" Meade asked.

"It doesn't matter." Gruen was wary. "Hannah's right. We're going."

"You're going to give us to the FBI."

"To me, Meade. What the hell do the feds know?"

"What about the money?" said Meade, standing up.

"What about it?" Gruen kept the barrel of the shotgun steady on Meade. "You thinking of making a deal?"

Meade sighed, "I don't make deals and neither do you, Sarge. Let's forget it."

"Where's the money, Meade?"

Meade nodded toward the rear of the cave. "It's hidden in the wall back there." He turned slowly and started along the rubblestrewn floor toward the money.

"Get it out, and let's get down the ladder. I can't pull a wall apart with hands like this."

After Meade had dug out the first brick, with Gruen

close by his shoulder, all that could be seen was the money in its neat wrappings. The top of the pile was still hidden by the adobe, although there was enough room to stick a hand into the hole.

"Jesus Christ, Meade." Gruen shook his head. "Saran Wrap?"

"Kids use it for condoms. It must be waterproof."

"Tell me about the dog. What kind of trick was that?"

"So you found him, huh? He always did like to lie down beside the road."

"But how could you have guessed I'd pass there?" Gruen asked.

"It was a gamble. I wanted you to know just where I was headed, because the border jump would have been great if I'd known you were there and couldn't stop me. You're the best in the business and I had to beat you. If you'd gotten too close, I'd have doubled back over to New Orleans or Florida. There are a lot of ways out of the country."

"Well, maybe next time," Gruen said gently. And then he saw the .45 in Meade's hand.

"No. Right now, Gruen. Drop the weapon." Meade cupped the butt of the pistol and pointed it directly at Gruen's chest, two feet from the muzzle. Gruen held steady, the shotgun on his hip angled at Meade. Hannah's clattering footsteps came from behind Gruen and he braced himself, thinking, goddamnit I'll kill him.

"I'll shoot, Sergeant. One man's already dead. I'm not going back. I'll just light you up right now." There was absolutely no emotion in Meade's voice. The game was moving to a purer plane, to a table of absolutes. Gruen felt the sweat stinging the rope burns on his palms. He stopped himself from shivering. Who was this desperate man? This wasn't what he'd wanted, no shoot-out like a cowboy movie, no final big rattle of death in the middle of nowhere.

"Oh, Christ, no," Hannah moaned.

"Think of her." Gruen jerked his head back toward the sound of Hannah's sobs. "Put the gun down, Meade."

"You think about her. Fuck it, I'm going to take you out, Gruen."

Gruen set the shotgun down, gently. The damn things were touchy if there was dirt in the mechanism. For a moment none of them moved. Hannah continued to cry. Meade held the .45 steady at Gruen's chest, patted down Gruen professionally, found his .38, and threw it over a wall.

"It's not worth it, Meade. Goddamn it, if you haven't learned that, you don't deserve to die yet. If you think money and escape is worth a killing, you're a stupid son of a bitch without any hope." Gruen took a handkerchief from his pocket and wrapped it around his throbbing hand. Meade said nothing. He motioned to Gruen to walk toward the front of the cave.

Gruen seethed. If Meade didn't kill him, he'd go back and tell the FBI the whole story. This man was a common crook, he deserved nothing better than to be hunted down by an army of people. His romantic belief that he and Meade were just a couple of old trackers playing a game was horseshit. Gruen vowed he'd see Meade in prison.

"Pack the money, Hannah," Meade said. He tossed the empty rucksack to her. She stumbled away, her mind numb. Meade cut a length of rope from a coil he'd taken out of the other pack, keeping the .45 trained on Gruen. "Lie on your side and put your hands behind your back, Gruen."

It felt almost good to lie down. Gruen wasn't surprised at the speed with which Meade trussed him. He just hoped that Meade didn't see the little tricks he'd pulled with his handkerchief around his hand. But Meade was in a furious mood of haste and purpose.

Hannah came back, dragging the heavy sack. Meade hunched his shoulders into it. "You can't leave him here, Meade. He'll die."

Meade looked at both of them. "Sarge, you seriously misjudged your old trooper. I wouldn't have shot. Hell, man, it would have been stupid anyway. I just drew to an inside straight. And you bought the bluff. And don't worry, I'll call the cops and tell them where you are when I'm clear. And your authority ends." Meade shooed Hannah over to the ladder and she swung over the edge and started down.

Gruen bided his time. The ropes were expertly tied with proper knots, he noticed. He should have figured Meade for the bluff. There were surprises in every business. And he believed him. "My authority ends, but I don't, Meade. Isn't that what you're supposed to be teaching the whole country?"

"Sergeant, you're the best there is and you know as well as I do that nobody learns anything unless they need to know it." Meade saluted properly and stiffly, smiled broadly, and disappeared down the ladder. His head popped back up again in an instant. "I almost forgot, Sarge, Merry Christmas. I won't be seeing you tomorrow."

In the little town of Arivaca, a few miles from the border, Meade broke the lock on the vestry door of Our Lady of Guadalupe church at 11:30 that night. He took a cassock (the kind favored by Spanish priests), a Bible, a rosary, a black leather satchel, and a square, lace cloth. He left five hundred dollars in a collection plate.

They made one more stop that night, in the desert. It took only ten minutes to dig the hole.

It took Gruen two hours to free himself. He had

slipped the balled-up handkerchief from his burned hand under the rope as Meade threw it tightly around his wrist. Fortunately he hadn't had much to drink, only the cup of coffee Hannah had held for him. When you were dehydrated, the tissues shrunk. It was not as painful as it was boring to lie there, trussed like a pig, working his wrist out of the ropes. He had a lot of time to think.

When he was free and had stretched his muscles, he made the long, swinging climb down the rope ladder. He was not surprised, when he reached the opposite side of the mesa, to find his car gone. He began the long trudge back toward the little store. Six miles of thinking of cold beer and where a bright little bluffer would try to cross the border on Christmas. Gruen had picked up a map Meade had left in the cliff house. It was a government topographical map, showing elevations, railroad lines, landmarks. Gruen noticed a smudge on the map, a fingerprint in adobe dust. It was near a cross in the tiny town of Arivaca. What the hell did that mean? Another joke, or was Meade up to something very different?

9

CROSSING

Nogales, Arizona, was a few streets of shuttered shops that sold hats, T-shirts, and turquoise curios of dubious quality, and thirty-two bars, all of them shut on Christmas morning. The town was wedged into the bare hillside above a wide dry wash, on the other side of which was Nogales, Sonora, Mexico, a similar town but one splashed with more ocher, containing even more bars and curio shops. The towns were connected by a bridge, with customs and immigration stations at both ends. A dozen wheezing buses were pulled up at the American side of the bridge and happy, holiday-dressed Mexicans, their arms loaded with presents, were creating a loud, joyful hubbub as they filed past the bored United States Customs men and passed through the gate onto the wooden footbridge that ran along the side of the auto bridge.

Church bells pealed everywhere, calling the faithful in for the glorious news of the birth. Fireworks popped, festive and bright on the Mexican side. Somewhere, an out-of-tune organ played selections from *The Messiah*.

A young priest, tall and slender-waisted, came out of a phone booth near the customs shed and picked up his satchel. A scrubbed young woman, wearing a lace scarf and high heels, walked with her arm through his, apparently chatting delightedly.

"What the hell did you tell them, Meade?" Hannah hissed through her smile.

"That their boyfriend was all tied up in archaeology. They'll be out there in a few minutes, and you can get off my ass about cruelty."

"You're cute in a skirt, uh, 'father.' " She pressed her breast against Meade's arm.

"Don't get fresh. Watch it now."

Meade and Hannah joined the long, happy line of Mexicans heading through United States Customs. The line shuffled along quickly. Meade sized up the Immigration men. Two young ones. Family men, probably begged off on the holiday. Not too experienced either, or they wouldn't have drawn Christmas duty. Both were flustered at the jostling, shouting, holiday throng who kept up an incessant babble in Spanish. A piece of cake.

"Merry Christmas, Father. Miss." The young man handed them each a day-visitor's card and waved them through. They walked quickly down the bridge, and Meade made the sign of blessing to several old women walking the other way on the bridge. United States arrivals were separated from him by a cyclone fence. It was mostly old women shuffling toward Arizona. They resembled those dolls made from wrinkled, dry apples in their black shawls and scarves and deeply lined faces.

The Mexico-bound line slowed. Going into Mexico for Mexicans was more complicated than leaving the United States. Identity cards were shown, forms signed.

Hannah and Meade waited patiently. They'd crossed the line painted on the rough wood of the bridge, separating the United States from Mexico. Meade saw in his mind an expanse of water, heard the creak of lines under sail, the plash of the prow cutting away from America.

"Oh, shit," Hannah moaned. "Look. It's him."

Sauntering toward them and the United States-bound walkway, one hand bandaged, wearing a blue suit and dazzling white shirt, was William Gruen. He stopped next to them and smiled through the fence. "Well, good morning, Father. Hi, Hannah. How's tricks?"

"Gruen, you bastard," Meade hissed, making the sign of the cross for a trembling old woman and smiling. "How the hell did you—"

"Such language, Father." Gruen kept his voice low. "If you cuss so much, I'll have to tell my Mexican friends over there at the border station that I don't think you're a priest. By the way, I'm glad you were in that phone booth. Gives me hope in humanity."

The line shuffled forward. The two big Mexican border guards looked professional and alert. They checked things thoroughly. Gruen kept a leisurely pace as Hannah and Meade neared the checkpoint.

"It wasn't nice to pull that .45 on me, Meade." Gruen was smiling. "Now I'm going to pay you back." There were only two people in front of Meade; they got through quickly.

Gruen stepped off the bridge and came around the guard hut to stand just behind the Mexican guards. The big Mexican took Meade's orange day pass, tipped his hat, and said in his best English, "Happy Chrissmast, Padre." The other guard took Hannah's card without looking at her, and the line behind them propelled them into Mexico.

Meade let his shoulders sag. Hannah's fingers dug into his arm. "You're letting us go?" she whispered at Gruen.

He nodded. "But I want a promise that you simply won't ever come back. It would be very embarrassing for me. The airline's money is insured. I've got to check out your story about someone being dead. I think the answer's in Missoula at the Brigadier's. Maybe when he knows you're in Mexico, he'll clear that up for me. I'll pick up the dog on my way back, Meade. We don't want to leave any pieces around."

"Why?" Meade was suspicious.

"Because, I just proved that I was better than you, kid."

"Oh, God." Hannah rolled her eyes at the hot blue of the sky and sauntered off to look at the flowers a little urchin was peddling in the dusty street. The bells pealed for joy, firecrackers exploded somewhere down a side street.

"Maybe next time you won't be."

"Maybe I'm not now, Meade. I'm letting you go. You've bluffed me again. I don't admire what you've done, but on a scale of one to ten, it's not much. And you're good. They won't stop looking for you: Interpol, a lot of volunteers after the money. You'll have to stay at it out there. All I'm doing, I guess, is throwing you to the wolves. But I think you'll last. Drop me a postcard when you get somewhere. And if you ever come back on my turf, it's over."

"*Vaya con Dios*, Sergeant." Meade put out his hand. Gruen, looking at it, looked at the black satchel this phony priest gripped in his calloused hand. He smiled and put out his big, bandaged paw and tenderly shook hands with Meade.

"The score is one-one, Meade, a draw," he said.

"Better make that two to one, Sarge." Meade lifted the priest's black satchel and opened it. Inside Gruen saw only a rope and a Bible. He looked up at Meade.

"I thought if I were caught at the border, I'd need some bargaining power; like, where is the money? I've got enough for a sailboat and one hell of an interesting surprise for the *Banco de Mexico*, being mailed down."

Gruen smiled. "You mean most of the money's hidden over there?" He nodded toward the United States side.

"Yep. Think you can find it, Sarge? I'll be back for it someday, you know. Oh, by the way," Meade fished his hand into the pocket of his cassock. "Here's your car key. Try to find out where it's parked, Sarge. That'll keep you busy until you get back across the bridge. Hang in there."

Meade took Hannah's arm and they walked away down the main street of Nogales, through the sunlight and the smoke from the fireworks.

Gruen began walking back toward the American side, refusing to second-guess himself. Suddenly he began to laugh. That bastard Meade had given him a set of General Motors keys. Gruen had been driving a Plymouth, a Chrysler car. If—no, *when* Meade came back for his money, Gruen wanted to be there. Just to say hello. *The Messiah* thundered away in a church on the edge of the wash, the sun baked everything in sight, creeping into the shadows, floating above the desert like a fiery parachute caught in the heavy air.